Her Hopes and Dreams

An Ardent Springs Novel

Her Hopes and Dreams

An Ardent Springs Novel

Terri Osburn

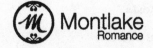

Published by Montlake Romance, Seattle

www.apub.com

Amazon, the Amazon logo, and Montlake Romance are trademarks of Amazon.com, Inc., or its affiliates.

ISBN-13: 9781503941427
ISBN-10: 1503941426

Cover design by Michael Rehder

Printed in the United States of America

For the soldiers—the ones who don't come back, and the ones who don't come back the same.

Chapter 1

Three days into life with her new neighbor and Carrie Farmer wanted to shove a tailpipe up the man's nose. Sideways.

The newcomer had no respect for the people around him. Though, technically, they were the only two houses for half a mile, so in reality, he had no respect for *her*. And he definitely didn't think twice about sleeping babies if the last two nights were any indication.

Enough was enough.

"I can do this," she muttered, stepping through her side gate to cross onto his property.

The farmhouse had sat vacant since Carrie moved in a year ago. She'd assumed the family who owned it would sell off the rest of the land one plot at a time, in sizes similar to the one she'd purchased. Thanks to a small life insurance policy on her deceased husband, Carrie had been able to put a modest single-wide trailer on her lot, and she'd enjoyed blissful peace and quiet ever since.

That peace and quiet no longer existed thanks to the jerk next door.

When she reached his porch, she fortified her resolve with several deep breaths. Confrontation made her nervous, for good reason. Seeking conflict wasn't Carrie's style, but this man had messed with her child, and that could not be ignored.

Plucking up the courage, she knocked on the door and then shuffled several steps backward. Nothing stirred inside. She knocked again. No response. What the heck? The red truck next to the house meant *someone* was home. Carrie moved down the porch to peer through a window, but the second she pinned her nose to the glass, a roaring engine shattered the silence. She nearly peed her pants as her heart threatened to beat right out of her chest. With clenched fists, she bit back the profanity dancing on the tip of her tongue. As Molly was on the cusp of talking, Carrie did her best to keep her language baby appropriate.

But dammit to hell, that thing was loud. Much louder than it had sounded through her trailer walls.

"This is ridiculous," she murmured, charging down the steps and around the side of the house. Nearly fifty yards away stood the scene of the crime—an old barn turned garage that did nothing to buffer the sound coming from inside. By the time Carrie reached the entrance, the noise cut off, and she hustled to take advantage of the quiet.

The dimness of the garage compared to the blinding September sun made seeing anything inside nearly impossible. One motorcycle hovered on a table to her right. Though, upon closer inspection, she realized the frame was empty. Clearly not the source of the problem. Another machine occupied the center of the space, and as her eyes adjusted, Carrie recognized a figure crouched down on the other side of it.

"Excuse me?" she said. "Can I have a word with you?"

Without getting up, a baritone voice said, "If you're looking for money, I don't have any. If you're recruiting for God, I've already punched my ticket to hell. Anything else, I'm not interested, so haul your scrawny ass back to the road and take a hike."

Undeterred, Carrie said, "I'm here to talk about that monstrosity that you're hiding behind."

Rising out of the shadows, he said, "Did you just insult my bike?"

Carrie swallowed hard. Dark eyes narrowed under full brows that matched the reddish-brown whiskers covering half his face. With slow, methodical movements, he wiped his hands on a dirty rag, causing the muscles along his shoulders to flex beneath stained white cotton. Years of living with her former husband had made Carrie an expert at recognizing danger. Keeping one eye on the looming giant, she scanned the area for a weapon, aware that without one, she didn't stand a chance against a man this size. His arms were larger than her thighs, for heaven's sake, and the rest of him was proportioned to match.

A crowbar leaned against the table to her right. She could probably get to it before he did.

"I'm not here to insult anything," she assured him, hoping her bravado would hold out. "But I have a baby next door who needs to be able to sleep through the night without that thing thundering to life at two in the morning."

Surely any reasonable person would feel bad about waking a baby. Then again, this bearded behemoth didn't look at all reasonable.

Instead of offering an apology, he stepped around the bike, his heavy boots thudding in the dirt with each step. Carrie scooted closer to the crowbar.

"Do I know you?" he asked.

"Like I said. I live next door. I'm sure you've seen me in the last few days."

He shook his head, releasing a long, wavy lock to hang over his right eye. "No, it's more than that. I've met you before."

As if she'd forget meeting a towering mass of muscle who bore an uncanny resemblance to a grizzly bear. "I don't think so."

"What's your name?"

"Carrie Farmer."

His eyes went wide. "As in Patch Farmer?"

Panic raced like a gas fire up her spine. "He was my husband."

"You're that married chick he was seeing the last time I was home."

"Excuse me?"

"I can't believe he married you."

The insult stung like a slap.

"Life is full of surprises," she said through gritted teeth. "Are you going to stop cranking this machine every night or not?"

He held up both hands in surrender, the rag dangling from callused fingers. "I get the message. I'll work on something else at night."

Satisfied, Carrie nodded. "Thank you. I won't bother you again."

"Hold up," he said, following her out of the garage. "Is the kid Patch's?"

This man took being a jerk to new levels. Without turning around, she replied, "Yes, she's Patch's baby. I was pregnant when he died last summer."

"Slow down." The moment his hand touched her wrist, she jerked away, spinning to protect herself.

"Don't touch me," she snapped.

"Whoa." Again he held his hands palm out. "I'm not going to hurt you, lady. Patch was my friend. I just want to know about his kid."

Reluctant to discuss Molly with this stranger, she asked, "If he was your friend, why weren't you at the funeral?"

His stance tensed. "Because I was stuck in a desert trying not to get my head blown off."

Recognition dawned. "Noah?" she said, trying to see the man beneath the beard. "Noah Winchester?"

"That's right."

She *had* met him before. Except he hadn't been anywhere near this size, and he'd been clean-shaven with the typical military buzz cut. Of course, he'd been an ass back then, too. Of all the people who could have moved in next door, why did it have to be one of Patch's friends?

Pointing out the obvious, she said, "You don't look like a guy in the military."

He tucked the rag in his back pocket, stretching the cotton over his broad chest. "The hair and beard were necessary to blend in for my last assignment. I got used to it, so I kept them after I got out."

"So you're living here permanently?" *Please say no. Please say no.*

"I am." *Of course he was.* "This house belonged to my grandparents. No one told me a piece of the land had been sold off."

"The trailer should have been a big clue," she said.

The hint of a grin drew her attention to his full lips. The top one curved like a perfect bow. She felt the urge to follow that curve with her fingertip.

Blinking, Carrie gave herself a mental slap. Where the heck had that come from? There would be no lip touching. Or anything else touching, for that matter.

"You interested in selling it back?" he asked.

Dragging her brain back to reality, she said, "Sell what back?"

"The land. I'd rather be out here by myself."

Of all the . . . She'd worked hard for this little piece of heaven, and she'd definitely earned it. Noah Winchester could blow it out his tailpipe if he thought she'd hand over her land so he could fire up his stupid toys whenever he wanted.

"This is my home. I'm not going anywhere."

Tucking the loose hair behind his ear, he sighed. "I was afraid you'd say that."

"I have no intention of bothering you again," she said, more than happy to give him his space, if not his land. "Keep the noise to the daylight hours and we won't ever have to talk again."

"Fine by me," he said. "But I have one request."

Carrie held the eye roll in check. She'd do just about anything to keep him out of her hair. "What's that?"

"I want to meet Patch's daughter."

Anything but that.

He'd never seen anyone go pale that quickly. It wasn't as if he'd asked to harvest the munchkin's organs or something.

"That isn't going to happen," she said, braced like a warrior ready for battle.

"Come on," he said. "He was my friend. I just want to see how his little girl turned out."

In truth, Noah wanted to see if the baby looked like her alleged father. The facts surrounding Patch's death had never made sense to him. The guy he knew wasn't stupid. And picking a fight with three assholes when he had no one to back him up qualified as all kinds of stupid. Something had to have set him off. Like finding out his wife was pregnant with another man's baby.

Still tense, Carrie said, "She isn't here right now. Some friends of mine took her for the afternoon."

"Doesn't have to be today," he answered. "I can wait." Curious, he said, "Did Patch really pick a fight with three guys in a bar, or did the story get exaggerated in the gossip lines?"

"He did." Ice-blue eyes stared out at the horizon. "Patch was drunk. I doubt he'd have done it otherwise."

"He had to have a reason," Noah pointed out. "Alcohol can make you stupid, but not that stupid."

With little emotion, she said, "Patch didn't need a reason to throw a punch. Especially when he was drinking."

Her tone didn't win her any points with Noah. "You don't sound all that broken up about it."

"Patch died more than a year ago. I had to move on."

Wrong answer. "The man was your husband. Did you even shed a tear, or had you already cut another guy from the herd and Patch did you a favor by taking himself out?"

Red shot up her neck. "Not that it's any of your business, but I was faithful to my husband until the day he died. I wept over his casket, and I'm doing the best I can to give his daughter a good life. You don't know me, and I don't know you. I suggest we keep it that way."

As she stomped away, Noah said, "I'll be around later if you want to stop back by with the baby."

Carrie froze, and he thought for sure she would march right back and tell him to go to hell. But she didn't. Instead, she slammed the gate on her white picket fence without looking back. Patch always had liked his women spunky. And she was pretty enough. In fact, unlike most women, Carrie Farmer had improved with age. She was still a tiny little thing. He'd almost hoped she would go for that crowbar in the garage. Would have been entertaining to watch her try to lift it.

Stirring her up probably wasn't the best idea. Noah had moved out here for peace and quiet. Something he desperately needed after how he'd spent the last few years. War zones were never quiet. And neither were his thoughts. The only time his brain ever shut down was when he worked on the bike. He needed the distraction like he needed oxygen.

Unfortunately, he also needed money. Custom Harley parts didn't come cheap. Strolling back to the garage, he hoped like hell the job his uncle had lined up for him would pan out. Noah had been swinging a hammer since his training-wheel days, and though the sounds of a job site would be potential triggers, he was determined to muscle his way through. In truth, he didn't have a choice. His bank account was shrinking fast, and Lowry Construction paid well for a small-town outfit.

With his late-night tinkering put on blocks, the night ahead was going to suck. He supposed it was time to check out Pop's library. If he couldn't lose himself in spark plugs and intake valves, maybe some old Louis L'Amour would do the trick. Meemaw used to send them in care packages when she was still alive. Trapped in some hellhole with sand stuck in places he didn't like to think about, those books had saved Noah's sanity more than once.

He didn't have much sanity left to save now, but he'd never been a quitter and wasn't about to start. Someday he'd get himself back to the land of the living. He'd definitely seen the land of the dying and wanted no part of that.

As he settled in behind the bike, Noah caught himself whistling for the first time in longer than he could remember. At the same moment, the image of flashing blue eyes filled his mind, coaxing a smile to his face. A man in search of distraction could do worse than finding a pretty girl living next door. Too bad the one across the fence had already broken Noah's number one rule. He didn't mess with cheaters. Period.

"A damn shame," he said to himself, reaching for a socket wrench with a whistle on his lips.

Carrie refused to be bullied. If she didn't want to introduce her daughter to the caveman next door, she didn't have to. The man had insulted her three times in less than ten minutes. Three times! She'd faced down plenty of judgment in her life, and willingly admitted her own part in bringing it on, but few people had ever had the nerve to spew their hateful opinions directly to her face.

What. A. Jerk.

Noah Winchester had been raised by wolves.

He'd called her "that married chick" as if she were a thing and not a person. Yes, she'd been married when she started seeing Patch. Carrie made no excuses for her behavior, but the only person she owed an apology was Spencer, and by some miracle, he'd forgiven her. Or at least admitted that they both had played a part in the bitter unraveling of their marriage. She'd been twenty-three when they'd lost Jeremy. The doctor had been adamant that there was no one to blame, but that baby had been in *her* body. She'd had one job—to keep him safe until he took his first breath. Only he never got to do that.

In the toughest times, she'd believed that her life with Patch was some kind of punishment. Penance for her sins or karma serving up justice for all her mistakes. Even during the rare moments when he'd been tender and sweet, guilt rushed in for all the nights she'd wished he wouldn't come home. The times she'd dreamed about running away to a place he'd never find her. Where he'd never hit her again.

But there had been no salvation waiting on the horizon, and though Carrie no longer had to fear a wayward backhand, other women were still suffering. Women who had no one to count on and nowhere to run. That's why she couldn't wait for the Safe Haven Women's Shelter to open its doors.

Earlier in the year, knowing that she possessed neither the skills nor the connections to establish a shelter on her own, Carrie had taken the idea to Haleigh Mitchner, her ob-gyn. That conversation had set the project into motion, and a small committee had spent the summer obtaining the funding needed to turn her dream into reality.

If all went to plan, by Christmas there would be a real option with advocates and protectors to stand between the victims and their abusers. Carrie had never found the courage to save herself, but now she had the power to help save others suffering from the same fate.

At the sound of a car in the drive, Carrie made a quick window check on the old barn. If Noah was still working, he probably wouldn't notice the new arrival. Or so she hoped.

Carrie met her company at the door, waving madly for Lorelei to hurry into the house.

"This child isn't light, you know," Lorelei said, carrying the baby's car seat in her left hand while the overstuffed diaper bag hung from her right shoulder. "What's the rush about?"

Without answering, Carrie took the car seat and dragged Lorelei into the house, closing and locking the door behind her.

"You are freaking me out, woman. What the hell?"

Peeking out the window again, Carrie said, "I met my neighbor today."

"The one making all the noise?" Lorelei asked. "Based on this reaction, I'm going to guess he's an ax murderer."

"No," Carrie replied, and then reconsidered her answer. "Well, I don't think so."

"Is he eighty and locks people in his basement? Or eighteen and running a meth lab in his bedroom? Because if it isn't either of those things, the only answer is that you've lost your ever-loving mind."

Setting the car seat on the couch, Carrie dropped down beside it to unbuckle her daughter. "He's a friend of Patch's."

Lorelei slowly lowered into the chair at the end of the coffee table. "Wow. What are the odds?"

"My thoughts exactly. It turns out this was all his grandparents' property, and he plans to live here permanently."

"Who is it? Do I know him?"

Carrie breathed in her daughter's scent while kissing her cheek. "I don't know. He's Patch's age, so he was a couple years ahead of you in school. I doubt you two ran in the same circles. Does the name Noah Winchester sound familiar?"

Squinting in thought, Lorelei said, "Granny used to play bridge with a Millie Winchester. She had a grandson in the Navy."

"Then that's him. We met a couple times back when I first started seeing Patch."

Doing the math, Lorelei said, "When you were still married to Spencer."

Lorelei had been Spencer's high school love, and the woman Carrie had spent most of her marriage being jealous of, regardless of the fact that her perceived rival had been living in Los Angeles at the time. By some twist of fate, Spencer's now fiancée had stumbled upon Patch smacking Carrie around on a downtown street more than a year ago and stepped in to save the battered woman. That same weekend, Patch died in a bar fight and Carrie's life had been turned upside down.

"Yes," she said, not proud of her actions. "Back then, Noah took issue with the fact that I was married and running around with his friend. Today, he asked if Molly is Patch's child, and he insinuated that maybe I'd been cheating on Patch when he died."

Lorelei leaned back in the chair. "Sounds like a nice guy. But what was the big deal about having to hurry into the house?"

Hugging the baby to her chest, Carrie confessed the problem. "He's insisting on meeting Molly. Says that Patch was his friend and he wants to see how his little girl turned out. As if she's a batch of cookies."

"And you don't want him to meet her?"

She didn't know how explain her reluctance. "Even after a year, Patch is like this specter that hovers in the shadows, waiting to pounce. I know he's gone, but the fear was so real for so long." Forcing her heart rate to slow, Carrie closed her eyes.

Lorelei shifted from the chair to the couch and placed her hand on Carrie's knee. "Honey, Patch Farmer is never going to hurt you ever again. No matter how many of his friends come out of the woodwork. But if this Noah person bothers you, then you have every right to tell him he isn't welcome around your daughter. You don't owe him anything."

"I'm afraid if he saw you pull up with Molly, that he'll come over wanting to meet her."

"Then I'll get out of here, and you make sure the doors are locked. If he comes knocking, ignore him. If he won't go away, call Dale. You know he'll come take care of this guy."

Dale Lambdon, a local police officer, had recently taken a romantic interest in Carrie, and though she'd had dinner with him several times, the spark simply wasn't there. Probably because he'd been the responding officer more than once when Carrie's neighbors had heard the commotion of another fight and called 911. Dale had seen the bruises. The split lips. And he'd heard the usual excuses—that she'd run into a door or fell down the steps.

In other words, he knew her weakness. And though he'd never brought it up in conversation, when she was with him, she still felt like the victim. The coward.

Carrie nodded. "I'll call him if anything happens. Maybe Noah won't come over at all. He made it clear that he'd prefer to be out here by himself. That doesn't sound like a guy who wants to be social."

"Either way, lock the doors and keep the phone close by, okay?" Lorelei gave Carrie a quick hug before dropping a kiss on Molly's forehead. "She ate an hour ago, and I changed her right before we left. She didn't nap for long, so I don't think you'll have a problem getting her down. There's a bottle already made in the diaper bag."

Following her friend to the door, Carrie said, "You're going to make a great mother someday."

"Do you think so?" she asked, doubt shadowing her dark blue eyes.

"I know so. Now get out of here before he sees your car."

"I'm going." Lorelei blew Molly one last kiss as she slid out the door.

After securing both locks and then checking the lock on the back door, Carrie peeked out to the garage again. The light was still on. With luck, he'd leave them alone. If they were going to live next to each other, he was likely to see Molly eventually. She would deal with that when the time came. Until then, Carrie would do everything possible to avoid him.

Chapter 2

Noah hadn't been surprised that his neighbor failed to pay him another visit the night before. Her reluctance to honor his request had been obvious, though he didn't see what the harm would be. All he wanted to do was say hi to the little bugger and possibly catch a glimpse of his old friend in the man's daughter. The funeral had come and gone long before Noah had heard the news. Years of watching his brothers-in-arms die way too young should have hardened him to the realities of death, but they hadn't. At least his fellow soldiers knew what they'd signed up for. No one wanted to die, but they'd willingly walked into the fray.

Poor Patch had been outnumbered and likely overserved. Maybe if Noah had been home, he'd have been there to back his friend up.

He parked his bike in the last spot next to the fence that surrounded the supply yard. If the size of the equipment was any indication, Lowry Construction didn't lack for work or capital. Propping his helmet on a mirror, he made his way to the entrance of the long metal building.

Stepping inside, he called out a hello, getting only silence in return. Blueprints covered the table to his right. The desk close to the back wall looked to be in use, though whoever occupied it was nowhere to be seen.

"Hello?" he called out again before checking the time on his cell. The text from his uncle had said to report at nine o'clock, and Noah was only five minutes early.

Assuming someone would show up soon, he slid the phone back into his pocket and perused the plans. The project appeared to be some kind of camp or dormitory, and if he was reading the lines right, most of the work would be cosmetic with a small addition on each end. Maybe Lowry wasn't working on the scale Noah had assumed. As he shifted the papers, a woman squealed behind him. Noah spun and braced for a fight.

To his surprise, his neighbor stared back, pale and wide-eyed.

"How did you find me?" she asked.

The question seemed a little vain. Showing interest in meeting her daughter didn't mean Noah would drive all over town looking for Carrie Farmer.

"I'm not here for you. I'm here for a job." Sounding harsher than intended, he added, "Do you work here?"

Ignoring his question, she shuffled to the desk at the back of the space, holding her tongue until the metal piece of furniture sat between them. "I didn't know Mike was hiring. Are you sure you're in the right place?"

"Lowry Construction?" he said, knowing full well that's what the sign on the building had read.

"That's us." Carrie hugged a delicate yellow sweater over her chest. "Like I said, I didn't know we had a new hire. There's coffee over on the cart. I'll call to see where Mike is."

"I don't need any coffee, thanks." Mrs. Farmer looked less than happy to see him. In fact, she looked downright agitated. "So are you the office girl?"

Jaw tight, her gloss-covered lips flattened into a thin line. "I'm the office *manager* of Lowry Construction. I run the schedules, track the jobs, and handle finances, including payroll. I also do human resources, which is why I'm surprised you're here. Are you sure this isn't just an interview?"

Unfazed by her tone, Noah smiled. "I'm sure."

"Right." Remaining on her feet, the glorified secretary appeared reluctant to take her eyes off of him. As if he might snap at any second and ransack the place. "Have a seat and I'll call Mike."

Noah did as suggested, pulling a chair away from the table. Remaining on her feet, Carrie dialed a number on the desk phone before reaching for a cell and typing in a text, all while keeping a close watch on her guest. A second later, a ring tone echoed from the office entrance.

"I'm here, Carrie," said a lanky fifty-something as he stepped into the building. "Noah Winchester?" he asked, crossing the space to the table.

Rising to his feet, Noah extended a hand. "Yes, sir."

"Nice to meet you. I'm Mike Lowry. Sorry I'm a little late." The business owner glanced at his watch. "Actually, I'm right on time. Have you been here long?"

With a shake of his head, he said, "No, sir. A couple minutes at most."

"Good." Turning to Carrie, Mike said, "Noah is going to be the foreman on the shelter job. I figure you two can handle the new-hire packet, and then we can all three head over to the job site."

"He's working on the shelter?" she asked, as Noah pondered why a secretary needed to accompany them to a job site.

"That's right." Mike moved closer to the table and shifted the blue-prints. "This is the Safe Haven Women's Shelter—or it will be when we're done with it. The original camp was built in the seventies and has been vacant for nearly a decade. I have a feeling the job won't be as simple as it looks, and if we're going to make the place operational by December first, I need a skilled leader at the helm."

Ten weeks seemed more than adequate to complete the work laid out before him. "I can handle it," Noah said.

"That's what your uncle Davis said. By the way"—Mike turned to face him—"thanks for your service. How does it feel to be a civilian again?"

Uncomfortable with the new topic, Noah shrugged. "I'll adjust. How many will be on my crew?"

"You'll have four besides you, and Carrie will be involved in most of the decisions beyond the initial construction phase, since this is as much her project as anyone's."

Now he was really confused. "With all due respect, why would we need a secretary on a job site?"

The woman in question huffed behind him, but Noah ignored her.

Mike narrowed his eyes. "Carrie is on the shelter board and has spearheaded the project from day one. But regardless of that fact, she's also an important part of this team, and if you're unable to work with a woman, this might not be the job for you."

There seemed to be more to Patch's widow than Noah thought. Sparing the tiny brunette a quick glance, he said, "I have nothing against working with a woman, Mr. Lowry. I meant no offense."

"Good to hear." Mike relaxed, but Noah could still feel Carrie boring holes through his back. He didn't give two shits what the secretary thought of him so long as she stayed out of his way. His new boss shuffled the blueprints into a pile and began rolling them. "Carrie, get Noah started on the paperwork, and then we'll head out."

"Can I talk to you for a second?" she said, ignoring her boss's command. "Alone?"

Sliding a rubber band around the plans, he said, "Right now?"

Carrie nodded, lips once again flattened. "Right now."

"Excuse us, Noah," he said, obliging the fidgety woman. "We'll be right back."

Something told Noah that this private conversation could mean trouble for him, but there wasn't much he could do about it.

"I'll be right here," he said, once again settling into a chair. "Ready whenever you are."

With one last look of disdain, Carrie stepped into a back room with her boss right behind her. Noah didn't know what he'd ever done to piss this chick off, but if she talked him out of this job, their silent-nights deal was off.

⁓

"I don't think this is a good idea," Carrie said as soon as she and Mike entered the break room. "There has to be someone else who can run this job."

"Everyone else is busy," Mike replied with confusion in his eyes. "What do you have against Noah Winchester?"

She didn't know how to answer, other than the fact that he made her uncomfortable, which wasn't a reason for Mike not to hire him.

"Why not put Brandon in charge of the shelter, and Noah can work on the parsonage?" Grace Methodist had finally gotten around to rebuilding their parsonage so the pastor and his family could move out of the trailer that was supposed to be a temporary home. "Noah could still have the job, but a different one."

"Brandon doesn't have the experience to run a project on his own. According to Noah's uncle, whom I've known since high school, he's the perfect choice to take the lead on this. I can't be in two places at once, and unless you want to push back the launch date on the shelter, this is our only option." Pouring himself a cup of coffee, he added, "Besides, he's a veteran who needs a job. I see no reason not to give him one."

Mike just had to throw in the vet part. And delaying the opening was not going to happen. "Are you sure there's no one else to lead this project?"

"Carrie, what's the problem? Do you know something about Noah that I don't?"

Defeat tasted stale on her tongue. "No, I don't know anything. I'll deal with him."

How, she didn't know. And the sudden pounding in her temples wasn't helping the situation.

"Are you sure? I didn't like his crack about a secretary on the job site, but he seemed to come around quick enough."

Carrie nodded, rubbing the tension from the back of her neck. "It's fine. I'd better get him started on the forms so we can get out of here."

Before she reached the doorway, Mike reassured her. "I wouldn't put him in charge if I didn't believe he was right for the job, Carrie. I know how important this shelter is to you. Together, the two of you can get those doors opened sooner rather than later."

The sooner the better for Carrie's peace of mind. She knew what it was like to be in a desperate situation and have nowhere to go. No other woman, at least not in the Ardent Springs area, should have to know that feeling. With a nod of agreement, she walked back into the office area to find Noah sitting where they'd left him, as promised. Pulling a new-hire packet from her file cabinet, she grabbed a pen from her desk and crossed the room.

"These are pretty self-explanatory," she said, opening the folder on the table in front of him. "I'll need either a passport or your license and social security card."

"Couldn't talk him out of it, huh?" he asked. The beard did nothing to hide the smug grin.

"Talk him out of what?"

"You don't want me on this job. Doesn't take a genius to know what that little chat was about."

If she denied as much, she'd be the liar he already believed her to be. And Carrie would not give him that satisfaction.

"Considering you accused me of cheating on my husband before he died, you're right. I don't want to work with you."

"It wouldn't have been the first time you cheated," he said.

Carrie didn't need a reminder of her past sins. "I'm not proud of everything I've done in my past, but making one mistake doesn't make me a bad person." Or so Lorelei constantly informed her. "I never lied to Patch. He knew from the moment we met that I was married to someone else."

Undaunted, Noah said, "But he isn't the one who broke a vow."

No. He just nearly broke her jaw.

"That's right," Carrie said, nearly snapping the pen in her grip, "he was nothing but an unwitting man swayed by the evil wiles of a woman. I'd forgotten that men are never held accountable for their own behavior." Dropping the pen onto the folder, she said, "Fill these out and bring them to me when you're done."

Without awaiting a reply, she stalked back to her desk, shaking with pent-up rage. How dare he sit in judgment? Noah Winchester had no idea what she'd endured at his *friend's* hand. The years of flying fists and unprovoked backhands. That had been the punishment for her infidelity. Karma had been swift and thorough where Carrie's sins were concerned.

Instead of screaming the truth of what Patch Farmer really was, she sat down at her desk and breathed through the anger. This was why she didn't talk about those years. Why she buried them in some deep, dark corner of her brain.

Hands shaking, she struggled to move the mouse where she wanted it. Taking a deep breath, Carrie focused on Molly's picture. The face of her baby always calmed her down. The drumbeat in her temple slowed as her cell phone vibrated. Crap. While she and Noah had waited in silence for Mike, Carrie had fired off a ranting text to Lorelei about her father's new hire. The message from Lorelei said that she'd straighten out the problem.

Carrie sent back a quick reply.

No need. Everything is fine. I'll call you later.

The message appeared to be too late as Mike's phone chimed on the other side of the wall. A few minutes later, her boss called her back into the break room.

"Are you going to tell me why the women in my life have it out for Noah Winchester?" he asked, brows raised. "What am I missing here?"

Refusing to let the past invade her present, Carrie kept her response short. "Patch and Noah were friends, and Noah and I don't get along well. Lorelei is just being protective because she knows that I don't like him."

"I can't *not* hire him because you don't like him," Mike said. "Maybe someone else on the board needs to take over as liaison."

"No," Carrie said. This was her project, and Noah would not take it away from her. "I can work with him. It'll be fine."

"Are you sure?" he asked.

"We're both adults. There's no reason we can't deal with each other. At least temporarily."

Mike nodded. "All right then. Let's see if he's finished the paperwork."

Carrie exited the break room in front of her boss to find Noah lingering around her desk. Her jaw clenched, but she kept moving. For the sake of the shelter, she would endure ten weeks with this self-righteous ass. Once the doors to Safe Haven were open, then she could tell him to go to hell.

Chapter 3

"I have my passport," he said, holding out the blue booklet along with the folder. "I filled in everything except the references, since that seems redundant at this point."

Nodding, Carrie took the documents. "Let me make a copy, and then I'll enter you in the computer later." She didn't meet his eye.

Guilt twisted in his chest, forcing Noah to admit that he'd crossed the line.

Once upon a time, Noah had put a ring on a pretty girl's finger, and she'd ditched him for someone else less than a month before the wedding. After he'd found them together in his bed. That experience tended to taint his perspective on the whole infidelity thing.

Back when Patch had hooked up with Carrie, he'd tried to talk his friend out of messing with her, but Patch wouldn't listen. The wedding ring hadn't even slowed him down. In fact, Patch had been determined to break up the marriage and have the pretty brunette for himself. A fact that Noah had conveniently ignored in his recent dealings with the man's widow.

The truth was, he owed the woman an apology.

"I was out of line a minute ago," he said before she turned away. "And last night. I shouldn't have brought up the cheating stuff."

Ice-blue eyes narrowed. "Is that your way of saying you're sorry?"

He'd never claimed to be good at the damn things. "I'm saying I know Patch wasn't an innocent bystander to what went down. You both knew what you were doing."

She hugged the folder to her chest. "And we were cheating. Together. So you still believe I'm a terrible person, but you shouldn't have mentioned it?"

"Why are you making this a big deal?" Noah crossed his arms. "I'm sorry. There. Are you happy?"

"Who wouldn't be with a heartfelt apology like that?" Carrie rolled her eyes as she turned toward the copier.

He'd said what he needed to say, and she could take or leave it. Not his problem. So why did he still feel like a jackass?

"Hey," he said when she returned. "Is that your little girl?" Noah pointed to a picture pinned to her pegboard.

"Yes, that's her," she replied, handing over the passport.

"Can I see it closer up?"

For a second, he thought she would refuse, but she finally removed the photo from the wall and handed it over. "It was taken about a month ago at a cookout."

"Who's the guy?" he asked. "Your boyfriend?"

He kept his tone more curious than accusatory.

"No, that's my friend Cooper. Molly loves to ride up on his shoulders like that."

Noah held the picture closer. "She has Patch's eyes."

Carrie agreed in a matter-of-fact tone. "Yes, she does. And her hair is darker like his."

"She looks happy."

"My friends make sure she has all the attention she could want, and Cooper treats her like a princess. Her first word was *Mom*, but her second was *Coopy*."

He handed the photo back. "I have some old pictures of Patch. I'll dig them out so she can have them."

Carrie's demeanor changed, as if he'd said something threatening. Her shoulders tensed and her jaw tightened. "That would be nice," she said. "There aren't many pictures around the house."

Noah got the distinct impression that she didn't like talking about her dead husband. To test the theory, he said, "Maybe we can share stories about him. Keep Patch's memory alive by remembering the good times."

She flinched as if he'd hit her.

"Are we ready to go?" Mike asked, joining them at the desk.

"Yep," she said with forced enthusiasm. "We're all set."

Mike turned Noah's way. "Do you want to follow us out there, or should we all ride together?"

"I'll drive myself," Carrie cut in, pulling her purse from a desk drawer. "I need to make a stop afterward."

Letting the woman have her escape, Noah said, "I'll follow you, if you don't mind."

His new boss nodded in agreement. "Fine with me. Let's go."

By the time Noah secured his helmet, the silver Cobalt had left the parking lot. As he fired up the Harley, he replayed their conversation. A grieving widow saddened at the mention of her deceased husband made sense. But that hadn't been grief in Carrie's eyes. She'd been more anxious than sad. A sensible man would leave things alone, but loyalty to his friend poked at Noah's psyche. There was something going on here, and for Patch's sake, he planned to find out what the little widow was hiding.

∽

Carrie fought the urge to call Lorelei on her way to the shelter. From the moment the other woman had kicked Patch Farmer hard enough to send him to his knees, she'd been standing between Carrie and the rest of the world. When Carrie had learned that Patch had been killed, Lorelei was there. When she didn't know where to turn or what to do, her new guardian angel had held her hand, helped her make calls, and even gave up her own job.

Before Carrie ran the office of Lowry Construction, Lorelei had been the one pulling numbers and tracking inventory.

All the more reason not to call. Her brief encounters with Noah Winchester reminded Carrie of something she'd been avoiding for more than a year. At some point, she would have to stand on her own. Lorelei couldn't fight her battles forever. With their wedding coming up in a few weeks, Lorelei and Spencer needed to focus on their new life together. One that didn't include an ex-wife in need of constant saving.

So Noah didn't think much of her. He wouldn't be the first, and she doubted he'd be the last. Lorelei had been right when she'd said that Patch would never hurt her again. Not unless she let him. Starting now, Carrie would no longer play the victim. Getting past the anxiety was nothing more than mind over matter. Lorelei had bought her a book on dealing with the sudden bouts of panic and racing thoughts, and Carrie had read it from cover to cover.

The author had provided several tools for maintaining control. Focus on her breathing. Find an object to ground herself. Self-talk her way out of the noise.

She'd been trying the techniques for months, and sometimes they even worked. The next ten weeks would offer the perfect opportunity for more practice. By the time the Safe Haven shelter opened for business, Carrie would be an expert at controlling her emotions. An endless source of calm. A virtual Zen master.

Or she'd have a permanent twitch and lose most of her hair.

Obviously, Zen would not be achieved anytime soon, but Carrie's headache had already faded, and the sight of the camp boosted her confidence. Less than six months ago, the shelter had been a wisp of a dream in the back of her mind. Today, thanks to Haleigh Rae Mitchner and her dauntless (and scary) mother, Meredith, who'd taken Carrie's vision and turned it into something attainable, they were on the brink of making it a reality. Now it was Carrie's turn to do her part and make sure that Safe Haven lived up to its name—providing a welcoming, safe, and free place for battered and abused women with no place else to go.

Parking her car in front of the main entrance, Carrie let the rush of possibility wash over her. This was her opportunity to make a difference. To do for others what she hadn't been able to do for herself. Though she wished differently, deep down, Carrie knew that if Patch were alive, she'd still be with him. Still allowing him to abuse her, physically and mentally. But maybe, if there were a real option, she'd have the courage to leave. Now she could give that option to others, and like it or not, she needed Noah Winchester to help make it happen.

The moment she opened her door, the sunny fall day erupted with the obnoxious rumble of Noah's motorcycle. He parked next to her passenger door and blessedly cut the engine. Finding Zen would be impossible with that machine around.

Mike pulled up beside Carrie's car and lowered the window in his passenger door. "We have a problem," he said, the truck still running.

"What is it?"

"Daryl tapped a gas line with the backhoe at the Methodist church. I have to get over there."

"But you have to show Noah around the camp."

The older man shook his head. "You'll have to do it. You know the plans as well as I do."

"You want me to do this . . . alone?"

"It's that or I try to find time this week, but the more we put it off, the later we start the job."

They were already on a tight schedule if they wanted to meet the December first deadline. "I can do it," she said, headache roaring to life. "Go do what you have to do. Will Noah's crew be here in the morning?"

"I've told them all to be here." Mike handed her the shelter plans through the window. "Get him up to speed, and call me if you need me."

As Mike backed out, Noah stepped up beside her. "Where's he going?"

Holding her purse in a death grip, she replied, "There's an emergency on another job site. I'll be showing you around."

"You?" Noah asked.

Marching toward the entrance, Carrie ignored the prickling along her skin. "That's right. Me. Let's get started."

∽

Noah was impressed. The little secretary—office manager, he corrected himself—knew her stuff.

"As you can see, the additions will require the most work, while the rest is predominantly cosmetic. Of course, the camp is forty years old, so there could be unforeseen issues, but we're optimistic that the job will go smoothly once we get started."

"That's the first rookie comment I've heard you make," he said. "No construction job, especially one on anything this old, goes smoothly."

Carrie appeared to be fighting for patience. "I prefer to be optimistic."

He wondered if she was this contrary with everyone or just him.

"So what's your stake in this?" he asked.

"Excuse me?" she said, stepping through a cobweb that would have sent men bigger than Noah squealing from the room.

Dodging the silk threads, he tested the sturdiness of a wall to find it detached at the bottom. Not a good sign.

"Why a women's shelter? Why not a kids' camp or something?"

"The area needs a shelter," she said, stopping near the entrance. "There are women being abused who have nowhere to go."

Noah didn't realize that domestic violence had become an issue in his hometown.

"Really?" he said. "In Ardent Springs?"

"Do you think men only beat their wives in big cities?" she asked, the color high in her cheeks. "It happens everywhere, and it's happening here."

Holding up his hands in surrender, he said, "No need to get so testy. Any man who hits a woman deserves to have his head knocked off. I'm with you. I just didn't realize we had that kind of a problem around here."

To his surprise, Carrie relaxed. "You don't believe in hitting a woman?"

What kind of a question was that? "Hell no, I'd never hit a woman. What kind of a guy do you think I am?"

"Women fall for men all the time who say that. A few months later, they're putting ice on a black eye."

This chick had clearly met some serious assholes before Patch.

"Real men don't beat women. Period."

"Even if the woman deserves it?" she asked, as if testing him.

"Never," he said. "Not even if she swings first."

Satisfied with his answer, Carrie smiled and her entire face changed. In an instant, Noah understood why Patch had been so determined to have her. Blue eyes brightened like polished diamonds, and a tiny dimple appeared in her left cheek. A man could search his whole life and never find such raw beauty and innocence staring back at him. Just looking at her made him feel lighter. More human.

"You should smile like that more often," he said, leaning against the wall, aware that a goofy grin slit his face.

"I smile at my daughter all the time," she said, her voice softer.

"Then that's one lucky little girl." He nearly asked if he could buy her lunch before he remembered who he was with. Noah shook his head to clear it as he rose off the wall. "Is that the whole tour then?"

Carrie's smile vanished, as if she too had come back to reality.

"Yes, we've gone over everything. The work starts tomorrow, and your crew will arrive by eight." All business once again, she held out the blueprints. "You can review these overnight if you'd like."

Taking the cardboard cylinder, he said, "I'll do that, thanks." An awkward silence fell between them, and Noah couldn't believe one smile had reduced him to a nervous schoolboy. "My cell number is in the paperwork back at the office. You can send it to the crew and make sure Mike has it in case he needs me."

"Of course. And I'll text you the names of the men you'll be working with so you know who to expect in the morning."

Good thing one of them was thinking straight.

"I appreciate that." Pushing the door open, he let Carrie exit first and caught a whiff of strawberry shampoo. His body reacted as if he'd never smelled a fruit before.

Thankfully, Carrie proceeded to her car without looking back, and Noah crossed to his bike, at which point he realized there was nowhere to put the blueprints.

Tapping on her passenger window, he held up the plans with raised brows. Carrie lowered the window.

"Did we forget something?"

Noah admitted his problem. "I can't get these home on the bike. Can you bring them over when you get home from work?"

"Oh." She looked down at her seat as if unsure how to answer. "I guess so."

"I appreciate it." He slid the cylinder through the window and stepped back. "I'll see you later, then."

Carrie nodded as the window went up. Seconds later, she disappeared down the gravel drive.

"Get your shit together, dickhead," he said to himself as he reached for his helmet. Seeing Carrie Farmer as anything more than a coworker, neighbor, and his friend's widow was out of the question. One pretty smile didn't change anything. Noah never made the same mistake twice, and this wasn't the time to start.

⁓

"I don't know what happened." Carrie perched on a stool in front of the Lulu's Corner Cafe counter inside Snow's Curiosity Shop. "He stopped looking at me like rotten garbage, and his lips curled into a grin. I think I might have batted my eyelashes."

Lorelei slid a cupcake across the counter. "You're only human, honey. Hormones had to kick in at some point."

"No," she argued. "Hormones do not need to kick in. Not now and not ever."

Thin brows shot up a flawless forehead. "That's a little unrealistic, don't you think?"

Carrie toyed with the cupcake wrapper. "Realistic is that I was unfaithful to one man and abused by the next. Clearly, my judgment is not to be trusted in either direction. I'm better off not getting involved with anyone. Not that I'd ever get involved with Noah Winchester. That would prove I'm insane."

"You aren't insane, Carrie. We all make mistakes, but that doesn't mean we don't deserve a second chance."

"This would be chance number three." She licked a dollop of buttercream off her finger. "Three strikes and you're out would be my luck."

"I thought I was the drama queen in this group." Lorelei waved a hand in the air. "Let's get Snow in on this."

"There's nothing to get Snow in on," Carrie said, but Lorelei ignored her.

"You need to help me talk some sense into our little friend here," she said as Snow took the stool next to Carrie's. "She's swearing off men for life."

"Been there, done that," Snow replied. "You see how far it got me."

Snow happened to be blissfully married to quite possibly the most gorgeous man that Carrie had ever met. Though Caleb didn't have arms like Noah's. *Not that arms matter,* scolded the one sensible voice left in her psyche. Which wasn't actually true. Arms totally mattered.

"Are you listening to us?" Lorelei asked, snapping her fingers in front of Carrie's face. "Where did you go?"

"I'm listening." Carrie sat up straighter. "What did you say?"

The shop owner laughed while the baker rolled her eyes. "Stop daydreaming about your neighbor."

"There's a neighbor?" Snow asked. "Why haven't I heard about this neighbor?"

"He *was* a jerk, but now he might not be," Lorelei explained. "And she's refusing to explore the possibilities."

"There are no possibilities. The man can barely stand the sight of me, and he talks about Patch like he was the greatest guy ever."

Leaning back, Snow said, "This guy knew your husband?"

Carrie nodded. "They grew up together. Noah was around when I first started seeing Patch. He knows that I was married and feels the need to remind me of my sins every chance he gets."

Turning to Lorelei, Snow said, "Why would we want her to explore anything with this idiot?"

"I'm not saying it has to be *this* idiot," Lorelei corrected, "but she's saying no man ever. That's a bit extreme, don't you think?"

Snow tapped her chin in contemplation. "I wouldn't say she needs a man in order to be happy. That idea has always annoyed me."

"Thank you," Carrie said. "I don't need a man."

"But," Snow continued, "you deserve a man who wants to make you happy. In fact, you deserve that more than anyone."

Lorelei pointed at Snow. "That's what I meant. You deserve a good guy."

"I walked away from a good guy."

"A guy that you're about to marry," Snow said to Lorelei. "Which always makes these conversations feel weird."

"There's nothing weird about it," Lorelei argued, which earned her two skeptical stares. "Okay, weirdness abounds, but forget the past. We're talking about the future here. A future with a man in it."

Dropping a hand on Carrie's arm, Snow said, "I've got this one. Lorelei. Honey. We understand that you want everyone to be as disgustingly happy as you are. We really do. And we love you for it. But you've got to chill out, girlfriend. I know that's a tall order with the wedding right around the corner, but try. For us. What do you say?"

"But she—" Snow held up a hand, cutting off Lorelei's argument. Surrendering, she turned to Carrie. "Just promise me one thing. Never say never."

Considering she was only thirty, Carrie didn't think that was too much to ask. "How about this? Maybe, someday, far off in the future," she specified, "if I meet the right guy, I'll think about giving him a chance."

Lorelei threw her hands in the air while Snow cracked up laughing.

"Speaking of the wedding," Carrie said, "does the shower still start at one on Saturday?"

"Yep," Snow answered. "Inside the newly renovated lobby of the Ruby Theater. In addition, or in lieu of gifts, donations to the cause are appreciated."

A one-screen movie house that a year ago had been on the verge of being condemned, the Ruby Theater had been saved by a group of locals, including Lorelei and Spencer, who'd dedicated countless hours to the cause. It was only right that they launch their marriage in epic renovated-theater style. Especially since Lorelei had chased the acting dream for a dozen years before returning to town.

Though the theater had been cosmetically and structurally restored, they still lacked the funds for the technology needed to make the screen operational again. For now, the owners had granted the restoration committee permission to rent the space for social functions.

"Then I'll be there at noon to help decorate." Carrie collected her purse and nibbled-on cupcake. "I need to get back to the office."

"Hey," Lorelei said. "Never say never."

If nothing else, Carrie admired Lorelei's optimistic outlook. Especially considering her less-than-positive past where Ardent Springs was concerned.

"I agreed to 'someday, maybe.' That's as good as you'll get."

Carrie could still hear Lorelei fussing behind her as the bells jingled over her head. *Someday, maybe,* she repeated in her mind. Even that seemed far-fetched at the moment. And then she climbed into her car and spotted the shelter blueprints on her passenger seat. "Don't even think about it," she muttered, securing the cupcake in a cup holder before starting the car.

Chapter 4

After a lengthy shelter meeting with Meredith Mitchner, racing to pick up Molly before the church day care closed, and then stopping for diapers and a replacement teether for the one mysteriously lost in her backseat, Carrie nearly forgot to deliver the blueprints to Noah. When she did remember, seven o'clock had come and gone and Molly slept soundly in her crib. Thanks to having the outgoing messages with Noah's number still in her phone, Carrie tried to call him to come get the plans. And because the universe hated her, he didn't answer.

Noah needed the blueprints to be ready for the job first thing in the morning. She had assured Meredith no fewer than three times that the work would start immediately and the target date would be met with no problem. Carrie would rather have her kneecap removed without anesthesia than face the wrath of the Mitchner matriarch because she hadn't sprinted across a yard to deliver some rolled-up sheets of paper.

But what if Molly woke up while she was gone? Not that she'd be gone long. And Molly was sound asleep. As her maternal instincts warred with her fear of Meredith, Carrie spotted the baby monitor. Those things had a really long reach, right? She could carry it with her, and if Molly woke up, Carrie could rush back.

Clipping the monitor to her jeans pocket, she grabbed her keys and hurried to retrieve the plans from the car. Cylinder in hand, she high-stepped through the damp grass, leaving the gate open behind her, and headed for Noah's front door. When he didn't answer, she faced another dilemma. His porch wasn't far from Molly's room at this end of the trailer. But if Noah wasn't inside, he was likely in the barn out back, which was a greater distance.

Committed to the mission, Carrie jogged off the porch and around the house. The sun painted orange and gold stripes along the horizon line, but it did nothing to illuminate her path. As she approached the barn entrance, loud rock music filled the air. Carrie could barely make out the words, which the lead singer screamed with brutal intensity. One line of the chorus came through loud and clear.

Something about middle fingers and not giving a fuck. Nice.

Raw aggression mixed with a heavy beat created a sound that fit Noah perfectly. Except when he smiled. He wasn't nearly as scary when he smiled.

Stepping into the dim glow of two hanging bulbs, Carrie found Noah with his back to the door. She yelled his name, but the volume on the radio had her beat by several decibels. Knocking on the inside of the large swinging door didn't help either. Seeing no other option, Carrie stepped forward to tap him on the shoulder, but the moment her finger connected with solid muscle, the man spun around and slammed a forearm across her throat, lifting her off the ground and propelling her backward. He moved with her, eyes wild as her back hit the one closed door.

Carrie dropped the plans to claw at the arm cutting off her air supply. She tried to cry out, but her voice box produced nothing. Noah panted, brown eyes unblinking behind the strands of dark hair covering half his face. The moment fire raced through her starving lungs, the arm dropped away and Noah backpedaled, stopping when he reached the far wall, and then dropping to the ground.

Dragging in giant gulps of air, Carrie's brain screamed for her to run, but she needed working lungs to do that. Chest burning, she lifted her eyes to see Noah still huddled on the dirt floor, his entire body shaking. This wasn't the action of an angry man. Carrie had seen rage and brutality. This was something different. In fact, Noah looked as traumatized as she felt. Searching the area for the source of the noise, she spotted a small speaker on the workbench to her right. Carrie yanked the short black cord out of the player, and the music cut off.

Blessed silence. And then she heard it. Crying.

Against the back wall, Noah's head hung low between his knees as his entire body rocked forward and back. Without thinking, Carrie closed the distance between them, stopping just out of his reach.

"Noah?" she said, her voice low and soothing. "Noah, it's okay. I'm okay."

His head shook, sending thick locks swinging.

"I shouldn't have surprised you," she said, recognizing the signs of PTSD. She'd read up on the disorder after several episodes of her own. Jumping at unexpected sounds. Experiencing intense fight-or-flight instincts, hers always taking the flight route. Clearly, Noah's instinct had gone the opposite way. Dropping to her knees, she leaned forward. "Take some deep breaths. In and out. Real slow."

Lifting his head, Noah shoved the hair out of his face and wiped his eyes. "Did I hurt you?"

Carrie would have a hard-to-explain bruise, and he'd scared several years off her life, but to her own surprise, she felt more like the attacker than the attackee.

"I'm sorry I startled you," she said. "I couldn't think of any other way to get your attention."

"Did I hurt you?" he asked again.

Running a hand along her throat, she said, "You cut off my air for a few seconds, but there's no permanent damage."

"Dammit," Noah mumbled, brown eyes lifting to the ceiling. "I thought I had it under control."

"You have a condition, Noah. You didn't know what you were doing."

"How do you know that?" he asked, straightening a leg past her knee.

Learning his secret didn't mean she had to share her own. "I've done some research in preparation for opening the shelter."

"I suppose getting knocked around by some asshole could leave a person shell-shocked."

To put it lightly.

Carrie rested a hand on his shin. "Are you okay?"

Heavy brows drew together. "Why are you still here? Why didn't you run? I tried to kill you."

A reality she didn't want to think about. There had been times, in the months before Patch had died, when Carrie had truly feared for her life. While dangling in Noah's grip, she'd revisited that fear. A fact that had her asking the same questions of herself.

"I don't know," she said with total honesty. "You were shaking. I couldn't leave you like that."

"You need to learn some self-preservation skills." Noah held out a hand, but she wasn't sure what to do with it. "I promise I won't hurt you again," he said. "You can trust me."

Despite what had just happened, she believed him. Carrie pressed her palm against his and was lifted off the floor as he rose to his feet. They stood less than a foot apart, dust swirling around them. Noah lowered his head and trailed a finger down her throat.

"That's going to bruise," he said, voice filled with remorse. "I'd never hurt you on purpose. You have to know that."

Nodding, Carrie murmured, "I know." Which made no sense at all. He had hurt her. And yet, she wasn't afraid of him. In fact, she didn't want to leave him. Not with anguish and regret still clouding his eyes. With a smile, she said, "The next time, I'll keep my distance and throw something at your head."

A callused thumb traced along her jawline. "God, I love that smile," he said. "I really am sorry, Carrie. I'm sorry you had to see that side of me."

"I'm sorry you had to go through something that turned you into that." She wrapped a gentle hand around his wrist. "The scars that people don't see are the hardest ones to heal."

"Do they ever heal?" he asked, eyes dropping to her lips.

"I hope so," she replied as his head lowered to hers. Carrie's heart sped with anticipation as his hand caressed her cheek. His breath feathered across her lips less than a second before a baby's cry filled the night.

Carrie sprung backward. "Oh my God. Molly."

"Where is she?" Noah asked, confused by the crying that sounded as if it were coming through an old radio.

"She's in bed." Picking up what looked like a white walkie-talkie, she said, "I have to go." On her way to the door, she pointed toward something on the floor. "The plans for the shelter are over there by the bench. That's why I came down here."

"I'll get them," he replied. "Go get your little girl."

"I'm sorry," she said, though Noah couldn't be sure what the apology was for.

Sorry that she'd come down here? Sorry that she had to leave? Either way, the crying tot had saved them both from making a big mistake.

Noah lifted the plans off the floor before crossing to the doorway to watch Carrie hurry through her side gate. He hadn't lost control like that since going off the meds. Guess he hadn't come as far as he'd thought. Her neck would be two shades of purple by morning, and yet, she'd treated him as the victim, not the lunatic who'd tried to kill her. Compassion mixed with that smile had acted like a magnet, pulling him to her.

That was the downside to avoiding people. A man had needs, and at some point, his hand didn't cut it anymore. That's what this sudden attraction to Carrie had to be about—basic human needs. She was the first woman he'd had extended contact with in months. The same would have happened no matter who lived next door. Only Carrie wasn't just anyone. She was his friend's widow and a woman with a history of infidelity.

Two immediate strikes against her. Their new working relationship qualified as strike three, and that meant Noah would be keeping his bat in his pants for the foreseeable future. He also needed to work on his metaphors.

The hit of adrenaline continued to simmer through his bloodstream, so Noah decided to call it a night. He had blueprints to review. After retrieving his phone, he switched off the lights and made his way back to the house. It wasn't until he'd grabbed a soda from the fridge and found himself horizontal on the old hand-me-down couch that Noah realized he still had Carrie on the brain.

Could still smell her sweet shampoo. Feel the heat of her palm against his. Taste her breath on his lips.

"Well, shit," he grumbled, sitting up. After running a hand through his hair, he took a long draw from the plastic bottle and tried to clear his mind. "She isn't for you, man," he said aloud. "You've got enough problems already."

Moving from the couch to the kitchen, he spread the blueprints across the table. With this job done as soon as possible, he could sever any ties with the woman next door. Out of sight, out of mind, right? Two minutes into the review, Noah wanted to growl in frustration. The project had a ten-week deadline. He wanted it done in eight. Based on the plans, they'd be lucky to open the doors after the first of the year.

It was times like these that Noah wished he still drank something a hell of a lot harder than the carbonated stuff in his hand.

Molly had not been traumatized by waking to find her mother missing. In fact, she had no idea that Carrie hadn't been in the next room. Her mother, however, had yet to recover. Four days had passed since the encounter in the barn. The encounter that had gone from terrifying to heart-wrenching to oddly comforting. If she let her mind wander back to that night, Carrie could still feel the tingle on her lips from the almost kiss.

Discovering Noah's secret had changed everything. One minute he'd been the big, scary neighbor passing judgment on the sinner next door, and in the blink of an eye, or rather, the blur of a choke hold, he'd become a kindred spirit. Though, looking back, the transition had begun earlier in the day. Not that finding a man adamantly opposed to domestic violence equated to finding a unicorn with a pot of gold or the perfect butt-lifting pair of jeans, but the revelation felt monumental all the same. Likely because, as a friend of Patch, Noah, deservedly or not, suffered from guilt by association.

At least in Carrie's mind.

As much as she loved her friends, none of them understood what she'd endured. Their lives weren't perfect, but, lucky for them, had been free of the kind of violence Carrie had witnessed and endured from a young age. The few years with Spencer had been a respite, until she'd lost their baby and spiraled into an abyss of blame and anger, all aimed at herself. Losing Jeremy had confirmed the truth—Spencer had been too good for her. She'd clearly never deserved him. She couldn't even carry a baby to term without her body betraying them all.

The moment the doctor announced that Jeremy had died—been strangled by the very lifeline that connected them—the soul-sucking soundtrack of her life had echoed in Carrie's ears.

You're nothing but a useless piece of trash.

No one will ever want you.

Why can't you ever do anything right?

Sabotaging the marriage had been the logical next step. She hadn't possessed the strength to walk away, so she gave Spencer a reason to hate her. Patch had been the complete opposite of her husband. Where Spencer charmed, Patch's teasing bordered on mean. Her first husband smiled all the time, while Patch snarled and complained. In the end, she'd picked a man exactly like her father. A move that made her cringe at its predictability.

Even once the abuse had started, Carrie convinced herself that she deserved it. She was useless, after all. She'd lost a baby and cheated on her husband and burned the pancakes. And her penance had been the occasional black eye or busted lip. At her lowest, she even believed that she'd gotten off easy. Patch hadn't broken any of her bones or burned her with his smelly cigars. Those were the kinds of things her mother had faced. All the while making the same excuses Carrie had made for Patch.

Carrie wasn't that woman anymore. She would never again tolerate being any man's punching bag, but that didn't mean she could be trusted to pick a better man. Words cut as deeply as a razor blade. What if she chose someone who never touched her in anger, but sliced her self-esteem all the same? No, she'd stay single forever before letting herself wade into those waters again.

Much of her newfound fortitude had come from books. She didn't talk about her experiences, but reading about others and how they'd recovered gave her the strength to help herself.

And now she could give that strength to someone else.

Parking her car before the camp entrance, she cut the engine and watched Noah's crew file out of the building. She'd purposely planned this visit for lunchtime in order not to interrupt the work in progress. Though her trip to the barn hadn't been all bad, Carrie preferred not to repeat the experience. Hearing Molly's cry through the monitor had been as heart-stopping as Noah's outburst, and she didn't want to relive either. That meant doing this at a neutral location.

"Hey there," she said as Noah stepped out last. "Can I talk to you a minute?"

Understandably hesitant, he waved off the other workers. "You guys go ahead. I'll catch up." To Carrie he said, "Does Mike need something?"

Considering they hadn't seen each other since the night in the barn, he could have at least asked how she was. Or if Molly was okay.

"No, I'm not here on business. I have something for you." She leaned into the car and lifted a beige tote from the passenger seat. "These are for you."

Noah took the bag and spread the handles to peer inside. "Books?"

"Special books," she said. "They're on post-traumatic stress disorder."

"You brought me PTSD books?" he asked, sounding more annoyed than grateful.

"I thought they might help."

"Do you think there's anything about this shit that I don't know?" Noah shoved the bag at her chest. "I don't need your damn books."

Carrie grabbed the tote before it dropped to the ground. "Noah, I didn't mean to offend you."

Lowering his voice, he growled, "I'm not one of your battered women looking for a way out. My demons live inside my head." He tapped twice on his temple. "No book is going to change that."

"But there are ways to cope—"

"There are pills to take that turn you into a zombie. There are group meetings that remind you how pathetic you are. And there are doctors who don't know what the hell they're talking about or how to fix anything. Cope?" he snarled. "Try surviving one night with this noise in your head and we'll talk about coping."

Noah turned away, kicking up dust in his wake. Carrie stared after him, too stunned to speak, but before he reached his bike, she found her voice.

"Who do you think you are?" she asked, stomping across the gravel. "Do you think you're the only person living with demons? The only one fighting off memories and anxiety that steals your breath along with any inkling of peace? I live with that every day."

"Please," he said, reaching for his helmet. "You don't have a clue what this is like."

"Don't you dare dismiss me, Noah Winchester. Don't you dare tell me what I do and do not know."

"Fine," he said, turning to face her. "What do you know about trauma? What happened to you that makes you think you know anything about what I have?"

Simmering, she met his glare with one of her own. "I spent five years being beaten by my husband. Five years never knowing when the next punch would come. The next kick. The next neck-jerking tug on my hair. I became an expert at covering bruises with makeup so no one would know. I concocted an endless supply of excuses for why he did what he did. Why I deserved to be punished and how he didn't really mean to hurt me." Throwing the books at his feet, she said, "That's how I know about trauma. That's why I understood when you turned on me the other night. That's why I applied extra foundation to my neck every day since, to cover the mark you left there."

"Is that why you cheated on your first husband?" he asked. "Because he beat you?"

Amazed by his endless belief in a man who didn't deserve it, she said, "No. My first husband never touched me in anger. The man I was stupid enough to leave him for did. Do what you want with the books."

Holding the tears at bay, she walked away with her head held high. Carrie had never voiced any of the things she'd just said to Noah. Not to Lorelei. Not to anyone. The confession left her hollow, raw, and exposed. Now someone knew her secret. The whole ugly truth. And she felt as if she'd been battered all over again.

Without sparing Noah another glance, she got in her car and left him behind. Less than a mile later, she could no longer see the road. Finding a narrow dirt lane, she pulled off and cried until she couldn't breathe. The sobs racked her chest and left her lungs aching. By the time she regained control, the pressure and pain behind her eyes were nearly unbearable. Grabbing her phone, she sent Mike a text.

> Not feeling good. Girl problems. I'm going home.

The lie would keep him from calling or checking on her. Though, ironically, it wasn't a lie at all.

Chapter 5

Noah lingered on his porch swing for more than an hour watching Carrie's trailer. There was no question he'd go over. He should have gone after her when she'd driven away from the camp earlier in the day. Only then he'd been too angry to trust himself. Denial had come first. No way the man he knew would beat his wife. The man he'd called friend—drank with, ran with, laughed with. But then other memories surfaced. Patch's temper had been on display more than once in their younger days.

He'd kicked a dog for nothing more than stealing a chip from his plate. Thrown a hammer at his sister when she'd pushed him too far. Kyra had moved fast enough to save herself, and Patch had laughed it off, claiming he'd never meant to hit her. The last time Noah had spoken to his friend, Patch had been different. Bitter. Ranting that the world wouldn't give him a break. Noah related to the sentiment, stuck in a dust bowl on his fourth tour in five years, and every trip around, the world looked worse than before.

But Patch hadn't been stranded in a war zone. No one owned his ass and told him where to go or what to do. If he'd wanted a different life, all he had to do was wake up and make one. Go to school. Learn a skill. Chase a dream. The possibilities had always been there for the taking. Yet, Noah had commiserated with his friend. Agreed that life owed him something and, dammit, why wasn't it paying up? After the call, had Patch taken his anger out on Carrie? Had she paid the price instead?

Being seven thousand miles away should have been enough to keep his conscience clean, but the way he'd treated the young widow this week had been inexcusable. Proof that his decision to avoid human contact had been the right one. Noah and his faulty wiring needed to stay as far away from people as possible. Not easy with a coworker living thirty yards away.

As the sun faded behind the trees, a dim light glowed from Carrie's front window. On Monday, she'd visited him in the barn shortly after sunset and the toddler had been asleep, which meant this was likely Molly's bedtime. Noah didn't want to have this conversation where little ears could hear, even if the baby had no idea what they were discussing. Then again, he couldn't be sure that Carrie would hear him out, but that didn't mean he wouldn't try. He owed her an apology, and it was time to man up and deliver.

When he reached her front door, Noah faced a dilemma. If the baby *was* sleeping, would his knock wake her? In an effort to do the right thing, he tapped more than knocked. No noise came from inside. He tapped again, slightly harder. The door opened instantly, but no more than five inches.

"What do you want?" Carrie asked.

"I'd like to talk to you."

"I don't feel like talking."

"A couple minutes. That's all I need." A lie, but a harmless one.

Clearing her throat, Carrie stared at him through the narrow opening, her face shrouded in shadow. "Molly is asleep. You'll have to be quiet."

Noah nodded. "Not a problem."

The door swung open, and his hostess waved an arm for him to enter. He took three steps in and stopped at the end of a well-worn sofa. A collection of colorful toys occupied one end of the coffee table, while a black cat occupied the other. The feline blinked green eyes his way, but otherwise paid no mind to the visitor.

"You can sit," she said, taking a seat on the far end of the couch and pulling a square pillow tight against her chest. In the light of the table lamp, Noah noticed the swollen eyes and red nose.

"You've been crying."

"It happens," she said, looking away.

Unsure how to proceed, Noah remained standing. He wasn't the type to rehearse a speech beforehand, but he wished he'd made an exception tonight.

"I shouldn't have been such a dick," he started, regretting his choice of words as soon as they'd left his mouth. "Let me try that again."

"You didn't know," she interrupted. "I stuck my nose in your business when I shouldn't have. Lesson learned for both of us."

Noah paced the small space between the table and the muted television. "There's no excuse for how I treated you today."

Tucking her toes behind the pillow, Carrie said, "Would you be here if I hadn't told you my dirty little secret?"

"Don't call it that," he ordered. "There's nothing dirty about you."

She shook her head. "I'm still the woman who cheated on my husband, Noah. Whatever Patch did to me doesn't change that."

"What Patch did to you changes everything." He lowered onto the couch, his body perched on the edge as he fought to control his emotions. "Someone should have helped you."

A brittle laugh escaped her lips. "*I* should have helped me," she said. "Lord knows I had plenty of chances. I just never had the guts to get out."

"You had the guts to stay the other night," he pointed out. "After I'd hurt you."

Carrie shrugged. "You were worse off than I was."

"Don't do that," Noah said, turning his body to face her. "I could have hurt you again, but you stayed."

Their eyes locked, and she sighed. "I'm an expert on rage and anger. You weren't angry, Noah, you were scared. That's something else I know a lot about. As strongly as I've promised myself to never let another man hurt me, I've made another vow. To help people *like* me. I doubt you appreciate the comparison, but I saw something familiar in the man shivering in the dirt."

The description set his teeth on edge. Where she saw fear, he saw weakness.

"So that's what the shelter is about? Saving other women going through the same thing?"

"Yes," she admitted. "That's what the shelter is about."

He couldn't let go of the idea that no one had stepped up for her. "Did you ever tell anyone what was happening? Ask for help?"

"What difference does it make now? I told you, I should have helped myself."

"All those years," he pushed, "and not a single person saw what you were dealing with?"

Carrie raised her hands in frustration. "Yes, people had to know. I covered the bruises with makeup, but not everything can be hidden. Neighbors called the police more than once. They knew what was going on. And the police suspected, but I gave them all the predictable excuses, so there was nothing they could do. Why are you so determined to put this on someone else? No one could have changed things."

"I could have," he snapped. "If I'd been here . . ."

"You cannot be serious." Carrie dropped her feet to the floor and leaned forward. "You were on the other side of the world, and when you weren't, you didn't even like me. You wouldn't be here now if I hadn't told you the truth about Patch. In fact, I bet you didn't believe me, did you? I bet you thought that your good old friend Patch Farmer wouldn't hit a woman. I'm right, aren't I?"

Noah wasn't proud of his answer. "That isn't the guy I remember."

Setting the pillow between them, she said, "If it makes you feel any better, I didn't see it coming either. Not until it was too late." Carrie reached for the remote and turned off the TV. The cat swished its tail but seemed unfazed by the humans arguing in loud whispers. "I didn't tell you about Patch to make you feel guilty or to earn your pity. Actually, I hadn't planned on telling you at all. But I do understand what you're going through. Maybe not to the same extent, but I get it. Those books I gave you are mine. They helped me understand my problem, and I thought they might help you, too."

He'd nearly dropped the beige tote in the dumpster, but something had stopped him and he'd thrown it in his truck. "I went through them after lunch. I've already read a couple of them, but I'm willing to check out the others."

"Good," she said, flashing a hint of the smile that turned him inside out. "I'm happy to hear that. And if you ever want to talk, you know where to find me."

"I'm not much of a talker," he said, not wanting to give her any ideas about them becoming some kind of therapy mates.

"I never would have guessed."

The sarcasm was nearly as attractive as the smile. "I didn't figure you for a smart-ass."

"Guess I'm full of surprises today."

That she could make light of something so serious meant she'd come a lot farther than he had. Then again, he'd only learned the truth today. She'd lived with it a lot longer.

Silence fell between them, and Noah recognized a dangerous thought. He could easily talk to her for the rest of the night. Which meant it was time to go.

"I'll let you get back to your night," he said, rising to his feet. "And I have some reading to do."

Carrie followed him to the door. "We're a couple of wild and crazy kids on a Friday night, huh? Game shows and self-help books."

To Noah's surprise, he said, "Are you busy tomorrow?"

Blue eyes went wide. "I have a bridal shower for my friend Lorelei."

"Right." Of course she had plans. Normal people had friends, unlike him. "No problem."

"But I'm free tomorrow night," she said. "Why?"

His palms began to sweat, and he tucked them under his pits. "I thought I might fire up the grill. Toss on a couple of steaks. You could have one if you wanted."

Smooth, jackass. Real smooth.

"I like steak." The smile hit full wattage, shutting down his brain.

"Cool," he said, nodding. "Come over whenever you want."

"Molly goes to bed around seven, so how about five thirty? Will that work?"

This meant he'd finally get to meet the tot. With any luck, he wouldn't scare her. Maybe he should trim the beard, just in case.

"See you then." Noah rocked on his heels, forgetting for a second that he was supposed to be leaving. Returning to his senses, he reached for the doorknob at the same time she did. His hand closed over hers, the softness contrasting with his callused touch, and he liked the fact that she didn't pull away.

"Until tomorrow," she said, her voice a breathy whisper.

Lost in her eyes, Noah repeated the words. "Until tomorrow."

Several seconds passed before she said, "Noah?"

"Yeah?"

"You have to move or we can't open the door."

He moved aside, careful not to crush her bare toes with his work boots. "Sorry about that."

Carrie pulled the door open, and Noah stepped outside.

"Have a good night," she said.

"You too." He descended the stairs, turning back one last time before heading for the side gate. She remained in the doorway, a silhouette with the glow of the living room. Though he couldn't see it, Noah imagined her smiling across the distance.

That had gone better than expected. And it was a good thing she had something to do in the afternoon. He'd need the time to hit town and pick up some steaks.

"You look different," Lorelei said as she took Molly from Carrie's grasp. "Mike said you left work early yesterday. I expected a cranky woman today, not one smiling from ear to ear."

"I'm happy for you," she answered. "Of course I'm smiling."

"Uh-uh." Lorelei drilled through Carrie's skull with a determined glare. "I know that look, and it has nothing to do with me. Spill, sweet cheeks."

Carrie should have known that Lorelei's radar never took a day off. She popped the trunk to retrieve her friend's present. Though the couple had encouraged donations to the theater, most of the guests were likely to bring a small present along with their contributions. "Noah stopped by last night."

Blonde hair swung with the head tilt. "Why would a visit from the bogeyman next door put a smile on your face?"

Unsure how to explain, and having no intention of discussing Noah's private business, she said, "My assumptions about him were wrong."

"I thought you said he doesn't like you."

"I thought he didn't. Turns out we were both wrong about a few things." With the diaper bag on her shoulder and Lorelei's present in hand, Carrie dragged the collapsed walker out of the trunk and said, "Can you close that, please?" She didn't wait for Lorelei to agree, but spun on her heel and headed for the theater doors.

"Wait just a minute," Lorelei barked, slamming the trunk. "You can't stop there." She caught up, hefting Molly higher on her hip. "What happened last night?"

"We talked." Carrie stopped at the door, waiting for Lorelei to open it.

"Talked about what?" she asked, allowing Carrie to step through first.

Eyes adjusting to the dim theater lobby, she looked around for the gift table. "Where should I put this?" she asked, aware that evading the questions was driving Lorelei mad.

"Snow set up a table by the stairs." Spotting the silver tablecloth, Carrie marched that way. "You're doing this on purpose," Lorelei said, following behind her.

"Maybe." The table was empty but for one pretty blue box, which she assumed came from Snow. Carrie set her glittery bag next to the box and slid the diaper bag out of sight. "I'll help Snow while you chase Molly around in her walker. She's gotten fast, so be ready to run."

"You aren't going to tell me," Lorelei said. "I can't believe you aren't going to tell me."

"She isn't going to tell you what?" Snow asked, joining them with rolls of blue and silver crepe paper in hand. "Lorelei, did you see where I put those extra rolls of tape?"

"Noah stopped by to see Carrie last night, and now she's smiling like a woman with a secret. And she won't tell me why."

Snow wiggled her brows. "Good for you, girlfriend. On the man and on driving this one nuts by keeping mum."

"This is *my* day," Lorelei said, on the cusp of stomping her foot. "You aren't supposed to harass me today."

"Was that in a memo somewhere?" Snow asked, a conspiratorial grin on her face. "Did you get that message, Carrie?"

With a flick of her wrist, Carrie expanded the walker. "News to me." Reaching for her daughter, she said, "Time to set you free, munchkin."

As Carrie wrestled Molly's chubby little legs through the seat holes, the theater doors flew open. "Where's my sweet-faced cherub?" Rosie Pratchett exclaimed, barreling across the lobby in her larger-than-life way. "Granny hasn't seen you all week."

Once upon a time, Rosie had been a regular babysitter for Molly. Two months ago, Carrie had enrolled her daughter in the Little Lambs day care attached to the Methodist church, and the Pratchett matriarch had yet to forgive her for it.

The older woman showered Molly's forehead with kisses before straightening and addressing her granddaughter. "Why are you here?"

Lorelei stuttered. "I . . . It's my shower."

"Your shower doesn't start for another hour, young lady. How are these girls supposed to surprise you with their decorating talents if you're here the whole time they work?"

Seeing Lorelei speechless was such a rare occurrence that Carrie couldn't help but watch with amusement.

"I'm here now," the bride pointed out. "What am I supposed to do? Sit with my eyes closed for an hour?"

"Spencer is waiting for you outside with explicit instructions not to bring you back until exactly one o'clock."

"Granny, he's supposed to be helping Caleb build a deck."

Rosie planted her hands on her sizable hips. "I don't care what he's *supposed* to be doing. He's outside waiting for you, so scoot."

Carrie doubted Spencer had put up much of a fight when Rosie changed his plans. Between swinging a hammer in the afternoon sun or getting an extra hour with his fiancée, the choice had likely been an easy one. They'd planned the wedding in a mere six months, and the last several weeks had been a whirlwind of meetings and last-minute preparations that had monopolized much of Lorelei's time.

Following her grandmother's orders, the future Mrs. Boyd ambled to the exit with no further argument. Another rare occurrence.

Molly giggled and rolled over Carrie's toe as Rosie turned on the younger women. "Let's get a move on, ladies. We have decorations to hang."

The two party planners hopped into action while their supervisor navigated the baby away from the dessert display.

"Well?" Snow said, keeping her voice low as she handed a roll of paper to Carrie. "What's up with you and Noah?"

Seeing no reason to continue her evasion, she said, "We're having dinner tonight. At his place. He's making steaks on the grill."

Snow shoved a dark curl out of her eyes. "What happened to that swearing off men stuff?"

"I might have been a little hasty with that declaration," Carrie admitted. She never really wanted to stay single forever. Not that sharing a meal with Noah necessarily changed her relationship status. They were neighbors grilling out. Virtual strangers getting to know each other. And with a nine-month-old as chaperone, how romantic could things get? "It's only dinner."

"Dinner is how it always starts," Snow said, taping down one end of blue crepe paper and twisting it around the stair rail. "And you're eating alone. That's very intimate."

"Don't be silly," she said. "Molly will be with us."

"I have no doubt Rosie would be happy to change that."

Carrie contemplated the possibilities. If Rosie kept Molly for the night, would Noah think she saw this as a date? Would he get the impression she expected more than dinner and conversation? Did she want more than that?

"You're psyching yourself out," Snow said. "Don't overthink this, Carrie. Let the man make you dinner, see how he is with Molly, and then, if things go well, that's when you can start overanalyzing."

Twining the silver paper with the blue, she second-guessed the dinner. "I don't know if I can do this."

"Do what?" Snow moved from the stairs to the newly restored concession stand with Carrie on her heels. "You're eating steaks with a cute guy. Wait, he is cute, isn't he?"

Describing Noah as cute was like describing childbirth as mildly uncomfortable.

"Though he'd growl at the idea, I'd call him beautiful," she said. "Thick brown hair to his collar. Beard, but the tolerable kind. Not the off-the-grid type. Whiskey-colored eyes surrounded by long lashes that most women would kill for. Solid muscle and at least three tattoos that I've seen. But the best part is his smile. His face changes when he smiles. It softens. Most of the time he looks like a bear with a splinter in his paw, but when his lip curls in that crooked way he has, I can't help but smile back."

Ripping the paper, Carrie taped down the end and looked up to find Snow staring at her.

"What?"

"Oh, honey," she said, shaking her head. "You're in deep."

"No," Carrie tried to argue. "I was just . . ." But it was no use. She'd been a goner the moment he'd mentioned dinner. "What am I going to do?"

"I don't know," Snow admitted. "But by all that is holy, don't repeat that description to Lorelei, or she'll have you living happily ever after by the end of the year."

Chapter 6

Noah reminded himself that he'd faced down tougher challenges in his life. Basic training. Night patrols in Mosul. A pissed-off general who didn't like his daughter slumming in the lower ranks. So why was the simple task of grabbing groceries so freaking daunting?

He knew the answer, of course. Too many people. Too many sounds. Too many blind corners and unwanted opportunities to meet a familiar face. The latter would lead to small talk—something Noah hated—and questions about where he'd been and what he'd seen. As if he wanted to take that trip down memory lane. But until Harvey Brubaker's grocery store started a delivery service, this was the only way to stock the pantry. And at least his payoff for enduring this mission would be a pretty girl smiling at him over the best steak of her life.

Who'd have thought he'd ever be having dinner with Carrie Farmer? Noah remembered the night Patch had introduced him to his new girl. Petite but not without curves, the shy brunette had tucked herself tight against Patch's side and rested a hand on his chest. That's when Noah had spotted the ring, and the compliment balancing on the tip of his tongue melted away. Young, brash, and still eyeball deep in his own bitterness, he'd brushed off her friendly greeting and told his friend he could do better than dipping his wick in another man's piece.

What a self-righteous asshole he'd been. Patch hadn't talked to him for two weeks, breaking his silence the day before Noah shipped out. They both knew why he'd made the effort. Knew where Noah was headed, and that he might not come back. Or if he did, perhaps not in one piece.

"Is that Noah Winchester under there?" a feminine voice asked, approaching him near the meat counter. "I heard you were home, but I didn't know you'd gone lumberjack on us."

"It's me," he said. "How are you, Kyra?"

Patch's baby sister was no longer a baby. Dark curls teetered atop her head in a loose pile while green eyes assessed his body with enough raw female interest to make him more than a little uncomfortable. No matter her age, she'd always be the little girl who'd nagged Noah into pushing her on the swings or to give her a ride on his bike. That ride would feel very different with her pressed against him now.

"I'm good," she said. "All grown up, as you can see." Prancing around, she showed off the skirt that barely covered her bottom. "How long have you been home?"

"Not long," he replied. The butcher handed over his steaks, and Noah said, "Thanks, man."

"That's a lot of meat for one person," she pointed out. "But I'm sure it takes a lot of protein to get a body like that." The perusal slid down his frame once more, lingering in areas that didn't care whose baby sister she was.

"I hear you're married," Noah said.

Her smile faltered. "For a couple years now. Lenny is good to me." With a wink, she added, "Lets me do what I want."

He'd heard that as well. "How's your mom? I'm sorry I couldn't get home for the funeral. I didn't know until it was over."

Kyra shrugged. "You know Mama and how she doted on Patch. She's still moaning about how the Lord took her boy too soon. Like he died in some accident, when we all know what really happened. She'd be better if my brother's bitch of a widow would let her see her grand-baby, but Carrie can hardly be bothered to send so much as a picture."

Regardless of how he'd treated his wife, Patch's family deserved to know his daughter. "You guys don't get to see Molly?"

Green eyes went wide. "How do you know the kid's name?"

"Carrie and the baby live next door to me out on Granny's farm."

"Oh, that's right." Kyra tapped a blood-red nail on the handle of her cart. "She used the money from the life insurance to set up her little trailer. Mama should have gotten a piece of that pie, but, of course, the weeping widow kept it all for herself."

Knowing what she'd endured, and that she'd been pregnant when Patch died, Noah didn't blame Carrie for using the insurance money to make a home for her and her daughter. But there was no excuse for depriving a woman of her grandchild.

"When was the last time Althea saw the baby?" he asked.

Rolling her eyes in thought, she said, "Probably back in the summer. I think Mama ran into Carrie at the street festival they have downtown. If she's seen her since, I don't know about it."

Unless they'd changed it while he'd been gone, the Main Street Festival coincided with the Fourth of July holiday. Which meant Althea hadn't seen her granddaughter in nearly three months. Too long in Noah's estimation.

"So are you going to eat those steaks by yourself?" Kyra asked.

Noah opted not to reveal the identity of his dinner guest. "Not all at one time," he replied. "It was good to see you."

"What's your hurry?" Kyra cut off his exit and trailed a finger up his arm. "We should get together and . . . catch up. You know," she

57

said, voice low and sultry, "I always had the biggest crush on you. Of all Patch's friends, you were the hottest."

Cheap perfume attacked his senses as her body invaded his space. There was no easy way out of this.

"This isn't going to happen, Kyra. Lenny might not care, but I do."

Green eyes shifted from emerald heat to jade fire. "You'll get lonely eventually, Noah. And when you do, I might not be around. Don't make me wait too long."

Lifting the front wheels of her cart, he made himself a new path. "You always were too spoiled for your own good, little one." As she fumed, he added, "Tell your mom I said hello."

Noah could feel the angry glare on the back of his neck as he walked away. The woman could wait around all she wanted, but he wouldn't change his mind. No matter how lonely he got.

❦

By the time Lorelei opened her presents, Carrie had reached ninja-level mastery of avoiding the bride-to-be. The conversation with Snow had opened a corner of her brain that had been sealed shut more than a year ago. After Patch's death, Carrie had run through a gamut of emotions. Though she was not proud of the fact, relief had been the first. Followed closely by denial, fear, panic, and in the end, liberation.

In the throes of her toxic marriage, Carrie had imagined what freedom might feel like. Living with Patch had been akin to wearing a metal cage around her lungs that someone tightened a little bit more every day. There had been times she actually stopped breathing, unaware of the action until her chest burned for air. One wrong move was often the difference between peace and chaos. The wrong tone of voice. A split second of eye contact. A fork out of place. All infractions that could set off the storm.

But she didn't live in that place anymore. For the first time in her adult life, Carrie knew total autonomy. She answered to no one except the round little bundle of joy on the other side of the room. Jessi Rogers, a young mother who'd moved to town in the spring, bounced her six-month-old daughter, Emma, on her knee while Molly attempted to steal the rattle from the younger child's hand.

Carrie didn't know all the details, but once the truth came out that Mayor Jebediah Winkle, a prominent member of the local Baptist church and longtime married man, was Jessi's biological father, the less-than-popular politician had opted not to run for reelection. To everyone's surprise, he became a doting grandfather seemingly unconcerned with his fall from grace. And even more surprising, Mrs. Winkle had taken the whole thing in stride, often seen buying baby clothes in area shops.

"She's getting so big," Haleigh Mitchner said, joining Carrie near the dessert table. Dr. Mitchner had delivered Molly, which meant she knew as well as Carrie did how much the baby had grown. "The way she swings that thing around, I bet she'll be walking in no time."

Carrie wasn't ready for her daughter's mobility. She could barely keep up with her now.

"I'm in no hurry for that."

Lorelei dragged a sexy nightgown from the bag on her lap, eliciting laughter and bawdy comments from the gathered crowd.

"I'll bet ten bucks that's from her grandmother," Haleigh mumbled.

"No way," Carrie whispered. "My money is on Snow." But then she remembered that Snow's present had been wrapped in the pretty blue box.

Holding the small card in the air, Lorelei read aloud. "'To ensure that I get great-grandbabies within a year.' Not funny, Granny."

The scolding didn't faze Rosie in the least.

"Told you," Haleigh muttered. "So who's this new man I've heard about?"

Carrie nearly dropped her cupcake. "What man?"

"Snow said he sounds hot." To her gaping stare, Haleigh added, "Don't worry. She told me not to tell Lorelei."

"She shouldn't have told you."

"Why can't I know?" the doc asked. "I'm not the one trying to play Cupid with every single woman in town."

Turning back to the festivities, Carrie said, "She shouldn't have told you because there's nothing to tell."

"If that's true, why are you so defensive?"

Until she'd met Lorelei, Carrie had forgotten what having close friends felt like. Now she longed to go back to her antisocial ways.

"Okay," she admitted. "There might be something. Or there might not. The truth is, every sensible brain cell I have left is telling me to run the other way."

Haleigh reached for a cookie. "And what are your non-sensible brain cells telling you?"

"They're full of ideas. None that I'm willing to repeat aloud."

"I know which sounds more fun to me."

Carrie snorted. "You don't have my history."

"True," she agreed. "But I had plenty of reasons not to trust my own judgment. I'm guessing that's your hang-up as well."

"I can't make those same mistakes again," Carrie confessed. "I won't do that to me or to Molly."

Turning her back to the crowd, Haleigh held Carrie's gaze. "Not all men are the same. If Cooper has taught me anything, it's that our pasts don't have to dictate our futures. You know better so you do better. If this hot dude turns out to be a dud, then you walk away. But don't miss out on something because you were afraid to give it a chance."

With a sigh, Carrie toyed with the cupcake wrapper. "This is probably all for nothing. He didn't even like me a few days ago."

"How could anyone not like you? You're the sweetest person I know."

"He had a good reason." An angry cry drew Carrie's attention in time to see Molly smack Emma on the head. "Oh, Molly. No no no . . ." By the time she reached her daughter, Jessi had put more distance between the babies. "I'm so sorry," Carrie said.

Jessi waved off the apology. "She didn't hurt her."

"I don't know what got into her."

"A fit of temper is all. Emma wouldn't give up the toy, and Molly ran out of patience."

Carrie knew firsthand what a temper could do, and she had a sudden flash of Molly following in her father's footsteps.

Squatting down to her daughter's level, she said, "You never hit. Ever. That is not okay."

"I doubt she understands," Jessi offered. "She's just a baby."

"I don't care what she is, hitting is not acceptable."

"Dude, you need to relax. Really. No one was hurt."

Teetering on the edge of something she didn't recognize, Carrie said, "That isn't the point."

"Is everything okay?" Snow asked.

To Carrie's surprise, the entire party's focus turned to her as tears rolled down Molly's cheeks. "We're fine." She pulled her daughter from the walker. "We'd better go. She's tired, and I should put her down for a nap before dinner."

"Yeah. Sure. I'll get the diaper bag." Snow rushed off to the table by the stairs. On her way, she said, "Back to the gifts. Lorelei, there are two more by your chair."

Carrie hurried to the door, soothing Molly as she went.

"Are you sure you're all right?" Snow asked, handing over the bag. "Your face is really pale."

"I'm fine," Carrie protested. "Tell Lorelei I'm sorry I had to leave early."

"She'll understand. Call us if you need anything, okay?"

With a quick nod, Carrie shot through the exit. Once she had Molly buckled into her seat, she kissed the little girl's forehead. "Mommy's sorry, honey. Mommy's so sorry." Wiping away her own tears with the baby blanket, she took a deep breath. *Crap. I forgot the walker.* In no mood to return to the party, Carrie clicked off a quick text asking Snow to grab it. "Maybe we'll both take a nap when we get home. What do you say, kiddo? I think Mommy needs sleep as much as you do."

A fair assessment considering she'd barely averaged four hours a night for the last few months. Carrie checked the time on her phone. More than two hours before she'd agreed to be at Noah's. A nap wouldn't leave her much time to freshen up, but this wasn't really a date anyway, so what did it matter how she looked? Better messy hair than a short temper and unprovoked tears.

Exhaustion swept over her as if the burst of emotion had been too much for her system. Carrie yawned three times before they'd passed through downtown. "A nap is definitely in my future," she mumbled.

Chapter 7

By five thirty, Noah had the grill fired up and ready to go. The steaks wouldn't take long, so he planned to put them on once Carrie and Molly arrived, but the potatoes were wrapped and cooking away. At five forty-five, his guests had yet to show up. The silver Cobalt occupied her driveway, so he assumed she was over there. Ten minutes later, he debated knocking on her door. At six, he started replaying their conversation in his mind. She *had* agreed to come over. In fact, she'd set the time.

So where was she?

At six fifteen, he knocked. No answer. Another knock, louder this time, and a baby's cry came from inside. Damn. Did he wake her? Was that why they were late? The crying grew louder until the inside door flew open. Carrie held the tearful baby on her hip and squinted against the brightness flooding the dim interior.

"What is it?" she asked, her voice groggy and one side of her hair shoved up at a weird angle. "What do you need?"

"You said you'd be over at five thirty," he answered, wondering if he'd imagined the night before. "That was forty-five minutes ago."

Carrie spun to check the clock on the wall. "Oh my gosh. I fell asleep nearly three hours ago. I can't believe I didn't wake up."

Noah noticed a dark spot near the bottom of her shirt. "I think the baby might have sprung a leak."

Following his gaze, she lifted the little girl away from her body. "Oh, Molly, honey, you're soaked." She took two steps into the house before turning back. "I'm sorry. Give me fifteen minutes, okay? I need to get us both cleaned up."

"Take all the time you need," he said. "Or we can do this another night. It's no big deal."

"No no," she yelled as she disappeared around a corner. "Tonight is good. Fifteen minutes. Twenty tops."

"Like I said, take your time." Not sure if she could even hear him, he raised his voice. "I'll see you in a bit."

"We'll be there," came the response.

Stepping back, he realized she'd probably forgotten the door was open, so Noah pulled it shut before crossing back to his own house. Remembering the potatoes, he took them off the grill, sliding them into the kitchen oven and setting the dial to one hundred degrees to keep them warm. He'd planned to toast the bread while cooking the steaks, neither of which would take more than five or six minutes, which left him nothing to do but wait.

Waiting sucked.

Few civilians realized how much waiting soldiers did while deployed to the desert. Waiting to move from point A to point B. Waiting for orders. Waiting for something to blow and shatter the silence. Noah doubted there would ever again be a time when quiet didn't unnerve him. The quiet was just the calm before the storm.

He found more of the same upon returning home. Hours spent pacing a waiting room while the VA docs debated what to do with him. Days of lingering by the phone, unable to move on with his life until they gave him answers. And then months of following the protocol laid out in endless pamphlets and forms only to end up no different than when he'd started.

Elbow deep in a project or a book was the only time Noah managed to relax. When his brain had something to focus on other than what might be coming around the next corner or buried under the next rock, he could pretend the demons weren't there.

Turning on the stereo, he snagged a pile of mail he'd been ignoring off the coffee table and settled on the couch. The stack consisted of mostly ads and coupon fliers, but Noah froze when he reached the last envelope. Return address US Department of Veterans Affairs.

Leaning back, he tapped the envelope on his knee. Having taken this ride before, Noah knew the contents meant one of two things. The first option would drop him back into the cycle of false hope. The other would leave him hanging out on his own.

Noah shot to his feet to pace the nearly empty living room. The house had been cleaned out over the years—various relatives taking what they wanted, assuming the house would eventually be torn down. What he did have? The kitchen table, the couch and coffee table, plus the bed in one upstairs bedroom were his mother's castoffs. Lucky for him, her hoarder nature meant she never threw anything away, even when the item no longer held her interest.

Slapping the letter against his thigh, he paced to the side window that allowed a clear view of Carrie's trailer. Mother and child were nowhere in sight, which meant he had time to find out his fate. But did he want the answer poking around in his brain while he attempted to act normal in front of Carrie? He didn't even need time to think about that one.

Gathering the junk mail, he tossed it in the trash and left the VA piece on the kitchen counter, grabbing the steaks from the fridge before heading out the back door. If he put them on now, they should be close to done when Carrie showed up. Once the meat was on the rack, he returned to the kitchen to deal with the toast. A minute later he was back outside, slapping four buttered slices of Texas toast on the grill. As he lowered the lid once again, Carrie stepped around the corner of the house with Molly on her hip. Her hair had been tamed, and the baby sported a brand-new outfit that included the smallest white sweater that Noah had ever seen.

"We made it," she said, as Molly squirmed to get down. "I'm really sorry. I guess I needed that nap more than I knew."

"No problem," he lied. "I just put the steaks on, and the potatoes are staying warm inside."

She switched the baby to her other hip. "I meant to grab a dessert before leaving town, but the shower didn't end the way I expected, and it threw me off."

Carrie didn't elaborate, leaving Noah to wonder exactly how a bridal shower was supposed to end. "You didn't have to bring anything. Unless you wanted something special to drink. There's Coke and orange juice in the fridge."

"That's fine." Caving to the child, she lowered Molly to the grass. "Dang it. I forgot her bottle on the counter."

"I'll keep an eye on her," he offered, waving metal tongs toward her trailer. "Go ahead and get it."

Hesitant, she looked from him to Molly and back. "Are you sure?"

Noah closed the grill lid and set the tongs on the makeshift table he'd set up earlier. "Hey there, little one." He dropped to the ground beside the dark-haired child. "You good hanging with me for a couple minutes?" Molly squealed before grabbing his beard and yanking. Hard.

"Honey, no," Carrie said, reaching for the baby's hand.

"It's fine." Noah lifted his attacker into the air until she hovered above his head. "Can't reach me from up there, can you?" Molly giggled, kicking her legs with glee. "You like it up there." Turning her around, he brought the infant down to his lap and looked up to find her mother gaping at him. "What's that look for?"

"I just . . ." Carrie shook her head. "I didn't expect you to be so good with her."

"I like kids," he said, ignoring the tiny hand once again yanking on his beard. "But I'll need to get the steaks off in a minute, so you better grab that bottle."

"Okay. I'll be right back."

Watching her hustle across the yard, Noah noticed how well the jeans fit her curves. Whispering in the baby's ear, he said, "Your mom is really pretty." Molly cooed in agreement, or so Noah assumed. Spinning her to face him, he said, "I'm Noah. It's nice to finally meet you, Miss Molly." Blue eyes so much like her father's stared into his. "I'm hoping we can be friends." She wrapped a strand of his hair around her fingers, and he had no doubt that the rest of him would follow suit before the night was through.

"I thought Cooper was bad about spoiling her," Carrie said as Noah wheeled Molly around on the tricycle he'd dug out of the barn. "But you may have just knocked Uncle Coopy off his pedestal."

By the time they'd finished the meal, Molly had been antsy to get down and play, but Carrie was reluctant to let her crawl around in the grass. The child would put anything and everything straight into her mouth, and to a baby a bug was no different from a piece of candy. As a solution, Noah had fetched an old tricycle from the barn, given it a good cleaning, and then settled Molly on the seat. He had to hold her to make sure she didn't fall off, but Noah didn't seem to mind.

"I'll have to build a seat that will hold her up, but she's welcome to have it." He leaned the trike backward, lifting the front wheel off the ground, which sent Molly into fits of laughter.

"You don't have to put yourself out for us," she said, aware of the warmth spreading through her chest.

Noah shrugged. "I don't mind. I like tinkering with stuff like this."

Carrie hugged her sweater over her chest as she watched him play with her daughter. "Is that what you call what you do in there?" she asked, nodding toward the barn. "Tinkering?"

"For now." Molly held tight to the handlebars as Noah pushed her in a circle. "I'd like to get a business going. Custom bikes. Restorations. That sort of thing."

"Then you definitely need to meet Cooper. He owns a garage in town, but he also restores old cars. You two could probably talk for hours."

Glancing her way, Noah shielded his eyes from the setting sun with one hand. "You mention this guy a lot. Are you sure you two aren't more than friends?"

She laughed. "Considering he's marrying my gynecologist, I'm pretty sure." Debating her next words, she decided to reveal their real connection. "Cooper is my ex-husband's best friend, so I've known him for a long time."

"And he still talks to you?"

"We're *all* friends," she replied. His surprise set her on edge, but Carrie refused to ruin the evening by being defensive. "Spencer and I have let the past go. He's actually getting married in a couple weeks. It's going to be the event of the year."

"Wait." Noah lifted Molly off the trike and rose, stretching a painful kink out of his back. "You're invited to your ex-husband's wedding?"

"Actually, the bride tried to get me to be in it." That had been a two-month argument that Carrie still couldn't believe she'd won.

"We're talking about the guy you cheated on, right?"

Patience gone, Carrie leaned forward in her chair. "Yes. The man I cheated on. Believe it or not, Noah, you're the only person still holding that against me." She bolted from the chair and reached for the baby. "It's getting late. I'd better put her to bed."

"Hold on a minute."

"Thanks for dinner," she said, ignoring his protest. Molly reached for Noah, but Carrie kept moving.

This entire thing had obviously been a mistake. One bad decision, which she'd more than paid for, and Noah condemned her for life. Once a sinner always a sinner. Fine. He was entitled to his opinion, but she wasn't required to endure having it thrown in her face on a regular basis.

Five feet from her side gate, Carrie heard the sound of heavy footsteps behind her and picked up the pace.

Well, hell.

"Carrie, wait." Noah jogged after her, reaching the gate as she tried to close it between them. "Come on. I didn't mean that the way it sounded. I was surprised is all."

"Surprised that anyone could possibly overlook my shameful behavior?" she asked. "Or simply surprised that I have friends? Unfaithful harlot that I am."

She didn't have to be so dramatic about it. "I've been in his shoes, okay? I can't imagine being friends with the chick who screwed some other guy in my bed. So sue me for assuming your ex would hold a grudge. I know I do."

Jaw still tense, Carrie said, "That explains a lot."

"Look. I see the world through one lens. That's the only one I know. If a friend came to you and said her ex beat her but now they're friends, wouldn't you have a problem with that?"

"You know that isn't the same thing."

"You're right. It isn't." Noah ran a hand through his hair. The last hour had been the most normal one he'd had in years. He couldn't let it end like this. "I'm sorry. I didn't mean to be an ass."

Staring off in the distance, she took a deep breath before meeting his eyes. "You're getting better at this apology thing."

Relieved, he said, "I've had a lot of practice lately." Molly stuck a thumb in her mouth as she tucked her head against Carrie's neck. "Someone looks sleepy," he said, running a hand over soft black curls.

"It's nearly an hour past her bedtime. She'll be out before I turn off her light." Carrie rubbed the baby's back. "I'm sorry that a woman cheated on you, Noah, but I'm not her. What happened between me and Spencer was complicated, and I make no excuses for what I did, but he's forgiven me. We've moved on. Well," she sighed, "he's moved on, and I'm trying to do the same. I thought you might be able to help me do that, but I guess I was wrong."

Noah knew a little something about trying to move on himself.

"I don't know if I'm the person for that job, but I do know that the hour I just spent with you and your little girl is the best hour I've had in months. Maybe years. Give me another chance, Carrie."

Light brown hair danced in the breeze as she stared at the sky behind him. Holding his breath, Noah watched the debate play out in her eyes. Would his heartfelt plea be enough? Doubt tightened his chest. In a short amount of time, Carrie had become a lifeline for him. A source of calm, quieting the constant storm in his mind. He didn't want to depend that much on anyone, but he didn't want to go back to the docs and their numbing pills either.

"Would you like to come sit on the porch with me after she's asleep?" she asked, a hesitant smile teasing her lips. "I can use the monitor and be close if she wakes."

With a rush of relief, Noah said, "I'd like that. Flash the porch light when she's out, and I'll come over."

Carrie nodded. "I'll see you in a bit then."

"I'll be waiting."

Noah stayed at the gate until mother and child had disappeared into the trailer. Crossing to his porch, he took a seat on the swing so as not to miss the signal when it came. Five minutes later, he realized he'd been sitting in silence without the usual bedlam in his brain. No fidgeting. No unwanted memories exploiting the moment. Just normal, soul-healing silence.

The little ladies next door might be the miracle he needed. A week ago, Noah had been certain that solitude was his only solution. That the damage he'd sustained would keep him from ever feeling normal again. But maybe there was hope for him yet.

Chapter 8

Thanks to her extended nap, Molly hadn't been as easy to put to bed as Carrie had hoped. When they'd left Noah at the gate, the sun hovered just above the horizon line. Yet by the time her stubborn daughter had given up the fight, night had taken hold. One of the many perks of living so far from town was the abundance of stars visible on a clear night. Though the forecast called for rain in the morning, the clouds had yet to arrive, and like glitter drizzled over black velvet, the heavens glowed from every direction.

Surrendering to her girlish side, Carrie ducked into the bathroom to powder her nose. She also brushed her teeth. Lorelei would have been proud of the extra effort. One final check on Molly, who snored away in her crib, and Carrie tiptoed to the front door. She flicked the porch light three times and then stood in the doorway, not sure what to do with herself. Did she take a seat on the glider and wait? Or stay inside so as not to seem too eager? But if she stayed inside, Noah would have to knock, and that might wake Molly.

Outside was the clear winner. Not that she had to wait long. No sooner had the door closed behind her than Noah appeared at the base of the steps.

"Hi," she said, feeling like a preteen going on her first date.

"Hi," he said, taking the steps two at a time. "Is the little one out?"

"She is," Carrie replied, overwhelmed by Noah's size and scent. Her porch wasn't nearly as big as his. "Do you want to sit down?" she asked, gesturing toward the ancient glider wedged against the side railing.

"Sure." Instead of taking a seat, Noah continued to loom over her.

"Are you going to sit?" she asked.

"I'm waiting for you to sit first."

Who knew a gentleman lingered beneath that gruff attitude?

Carrie settled onto the teal cushion and shivered the moment cold metal touched her back. She should have skipped the toothpaste and taken the extra minute to find a jacket.

"Are you cold?" Noah asked, taking the seat beside her and stretching a strong arm along the back of the seat.

"I'll be okay," she assured him, shivering again.

"Here." He pulled her close against his side. The man was like a raging furnace. "Better?"

He had no idea. Carrie didn't trust her voice not to betray her, so she nodded instead.

"I forgot how clear the skies are out here," he said, his head resting on the back of the glider. You don't get this kind of a view in town. Or this kind of quiet either."

Nature seemed determined to make him a liar. Crickets and frogs filled the night with croaks and chirps. Something howled in the distance, and the leaves rustled in the wind.

"You call this quiet?" she asked.

Noah closed his eyes and nodded. "I do."

Following his lead, Carrie closed her own eyes and relaxed into him. "When I found this spot to put the trailer on, I thought I'd won the lottery. So pretty and free of nosy neighbors."

"And then I moved in next door," he said with a laugh. "I didn't know Mama had sold off a piece of the place until I got here."

"I assumed they'd sell off the rest," she said, staring up at the stars. "Why did they leave the house empty for so long?"

He raised his head to stare at his crossed ankles. "Granny left the place to me and my cousin Zeke. We both went into the military about the same time, and I guess she thought we'd need something to come home to."

"Does that mean Zeke will be moving in soon?" Carrie asked.

His big body tensed. "Zeke's Humvee hit an IED two years ago. No survivors."

Heart aching, she said, "I'm sorry. Now I'm the nosy neighbor."

"It's all right. A lot of guys didn't make it back."

Carrie whispered the first thought that came to mind. "I'm glad you did."

Noah relaxed, his solid thigh leaning against hers. "Sometimes I'm not so sure. I didn't come back the same."

"The scars can't change us unless we let them," she murmured. "You just need a little time to heal, Noah. Give yourself time."

Noah didn't respond, and they continued to enjoy the stars in silence. Carrie knew that he doubted her words, but she fought the urge to argue. To push him on a topic he clearly didn't like to talk about. After nearly a minute of listening to his even breathing, she found herself leaning into his side, more comfortable with a man than she'd been in a very long time.

"Thank you," he whispered into her hair.

Glancing up, she said, "For what?"

"For giving me peace."

Carrie narrowed her eyes. "Peace?" she asked. She'd done nothing but sit beside him.

He placed a kiss on the end of her nose. "Yeah. Peace."

∽

Noah hadn't felt this good in years.

His mind still raced, but explosions and carnage had been replaced by Carrie's trusting blue eyes and her soft curves. Remembering them pressed against his side was enough to short-circuit his brain. He'd been tempted to cross the line. To push his luck and pull her onto his lap. If she'd been any other woman, Noah might have made the advance. But Carrie deserved a little wooing, as his mother called it. He could do that. Show her how a real man treated a woman.

As he replayed the evening in his mind, Noah remembered the run-in with Kyra. Part of him figured she'd been lying. Playing her typical brat games, stirring up trouble where none existed. Still, he'd intended to ask about Carrie's relationship with her in-laws. But then Molly had yanked on his beard while Carrie flashed the easy smile that made him forget his name, and Patch's sister had faded into a distant memory.

An arm propped behind his head and a Louis L'Amour forgotten beside the bed, Noah stared at the ceiling while crickets created a chorus outside his window. Carrie had given him a lot to think about. Besides the future prospect of taking her to bed, there had been her belief that all he needed was time. For months he'd considered himself a lost cause. But Carrie didn't see him that way. She saw a man. A whole man with a few bumps and bruises, but nothing that couldn't be fixed.

God, he hoped she was right.

The night sounds faded as Noah's eyes grew heavy. For the first time in months, he drifted off to sleep without a struggle. As the hours passed, a pretty brunette with ice-blue eyes and delicate curves filled his dreams, but not for long. At dawn, he jerked awake, covered in sweat and huffing as if he'd run a four-minute mile. Shaken and naked, Noah stumbled to the bathroom to throw cold water on his face. Straightening, he caught his reflection in the mirror. Recognized the demons still dancing in his eyes. The ghosts lurking in the shadows behind him.

"More time," he mumbled, his voice still groggy from sleep. "Time isn't going to fix this."

⤬

Sleep had been impossible, and not because of her usual insomnia. Every time Carrie closed her eyes, she saw Noah smiling down at her. And by the wee hours of the morning she'd been imagining much more than a smile.

Carrie had never been the type to indulge in fantasies or imagine erotic escapades of any kind. Which made her sudden wayward thoughts all the more disturbing. By the time the sun crested her windowsill, she'd conjured up scenarios that would make Lorelei blush. And *nothing* made Lorelei blush. Even thinking about them stirred heat in places Carrie hadn't thought about in more than a year.

"I'm pretty sure you can go to hell for thinking that stuff inside a church," Mya said, jolting Carrie back to reality.

"I don't know what you're talking about," Carrie mumbled, returning her attention to the children's books she was stacking on a shelf. Molly had been cranky before church, so when Carrie found her sound asleep after the service ended, she decided to help clean up while the baby finished her nap.

"From one single woman to another, I know that look. You either installed new batteries, or there's been a development on the man front."

During her five months attending the church, Carrie had gotten to know Mya Reynolds due to her role as the primary caretaker in the Grace Methodist childcare room. Though Carrie hadn't been raised with any sort of religious affiliation, she wanted her daughter to have something akin to a normal upbringing. And in Ardent Springs, a normal upbringing included attending church regularly.

Open to the possibilities, Carrie had attended several different churches before settling on Grace Methodist. The congregation had been friendly and welcoming to the new little family, while the positive tone of the service always left her feeling a little lighter than when she'd walked in. This had not been her experience at some of the other options in town, which made her decision that much easier.

"I don't own anything that needs batteries," Carrie replied. Which was a lie, thanks to Lorelei, but she'd never taken it out of the box and therefore felt as if she were telling the truth, if only by a technicality. She silently pled the Fifth on the second suggestion.

During the week, Mya worked at the Ardent Springs Post Office, and as far as Carrie knew, she'd done so her entire adult life. A couple years older than Carrie, Mya had graduated high school with Cooper, Spencer, and Lorelei, but according to the latter she had been a book-worm who rarely spoke and almost never socialized. Carrie had never seen Mya not carrying a book around, and she suspected Mya's devotion to the childcare room during services indicated a continued disinterest in being social.

Mya had also been best friends with Dale Lambdon since childhood, which made this conversation all the more awkward.

Emptying an armload of toys into a storage bin, Mya said, "So who's the guy?"

The only person Carrie had spent any time with in the last four months had been Dale. Which meant Mya might know more than she let on.

"Why do you assume it isn't Dale?" she asked.

Green eyes held Carrie's gaze. "We both know that Dale has been barking up the wrong tree. Though I haven't been able to figure out why you let him keep barking."

Guilt twisted in her gut. "I thought if I gave it enough time that my feelings would change. He's such a great guy, you know? Any girl would be lucky to have him."

"I've been telling him that for years." Mya gathered three teddy bears and a stuffed lamb off the floor. "And every woman he dates proves me wrong. The man gets friend-zoned quicker than gossip runs from one end of this town to another. He's getting a complex."

"He'll find the right girl," Carrie said, sliding the last three books into place. "Eventually."

"At least warn me before you let him down so I can be ready. And whatever you do, don't use that 'it's not you it's me' crap when you do it." She snagged a fluffy lion out of a playpen. "He's heard that one enough already."

Carrie watched Mya thrust the stuffed animals on top of the other toys, recognizing a truth she'd overlooked until now. A truth that Mya quite possibly either didn't recognize herself, or chose not to admit.

"I'll be as kind as I can," Carrie assured her.

"So what about the wedding?" Mya asked.

The wedding. Crap. Carrie had agreed to go with Dale while Mya watched Molly. She couldn't back out on him now with less than two weeks to go. And though she loved her daughter, she also looked forward to an all-adult day free of diaper bags and teething rings.

"I don't know," she said. "I haven't thought that far ahead."

"There you are," said Dale as he stepped into the room at the exact wrong moment. "I didn't see you in the fellowship hall, so I figured you'd be back here." With a quick glance, he added, "Hey, My."

"Hey, Dale," the other woman said, giving Carrie a *don't you dare hurt him* look.

"Molly fell asleep during the service," she said. "I didn't want to wake her, so I opted to help Mya clean up the day care."

"That was nice of you." He smiled at Carrie as if she'd saved a gaggle of baby ducks.

"I just picked up a few books," she clarified. "Mya did most of the work."

Over Dale's shoulder, Carrie saw Mya roll her eyes.

"What are you doing next weekend?" Dale asked.

"Who, me?" she asked.

"No, Mya," he said with a laugh. "Yeah, you."

The other woman flinched, and Carrie wanted to smack Dale upside the head.

"This weekend is Lorelei's bachelorette party," she answered, relieved to have a valid excuse to be busy.

"That's Saturday, isn't it?" he asked.

"Yes, that's right."

"Then how about Friday night I take you to dinner? There's a new place down in Goodlettsville that I hear is good." Turning to Mya, he said, "You'll watch Molly, right?"

"I have plans on Friday night," she replied, crossing her arms.

"Oh." Dale turned back to Carrie. "We can stay here in town, then. Molly can come with us."

Hopeful that she'd have plans with Noah for Friday night, Carrie searched for an excuse. "I don't think so, Dale. Saturday is going to be crazy, and Molly's been really fussy from teething. I'll have to pass this time."

Dale slid his hands into his pockets, taking the rejection like the good guy he was. "No problem," he said. "It was just an idea. We're still on for the wedding, right?"

Mya shot Carrie a raised-brow look as if to say, *Now's your chance, woman.*

"Yes. Of course. We're still on for the wedding," she said, ignoring the woman throwing her hands in the air on the other side of the room. "A week from Saturday. As planned."

"Good," Dale said, rubbing his hands together. "I'm looking forward to it. The doughnuts are getting low up in the hall. Do you want me to bring you one?"

The offer didn't appear to extend to Mya. "None for me, thanks," Carrie said. "But Mya might want one."

Before the other woman could reply, Dale said, "Mya doesn't eat doughnuts. She swore off junk food three years ago."

"You don't have to talk about me like I'm not here," Mya snapped.

Instead of apologizing, he said, "And that's what swearing off doughnuts does to you. Makes you quick to anger."

A stuffed giraffe flew by his head as Molly stirred in her playpen. Carrie moved to retrieve her daughter as the pair continued their discussion.

"You're a jerk," Mya said.

"You're a health nut," Dale replied.

"That isn't an insult," she informed him.

"Spoken like a true health nut," he quipped.

These two needed to get a room and get on with it. Talk about clueless.

"I'm going back up front," Dale said to Carrie. "Want me to save you a seat?"

She shook her head. "I'm going to head on home." Home to see Noah, she admitted to herself. "But Mya can go with you now that the last baby is leaving."

Dale moaned. "She'll tell me all the horrible things the doughnut will do to my system."

"Maybe she tells you stuff like that because she cares about you," Carrie said as she slipped a pacifier into Molly's mouth. "Did you ever think of that?"

The delusional friends exchanged a dubious look.

"Do you care about me, Mya?" he asked with a teasing smile.

Mya didn't look like a woman who wanted to be teased. "You wish, goofball. Go get your doughnut. I'll be up in a minute."

With a gentle poke at Molly's nose, he said, "I hope your teeth stop giving you trouble, pretty girl." On his way out the door, Dale stuck his tongue out at Mya, who ignored him.

Carrie gathered Molly's things together and draped a blanket over her daughter. Before leaving, she said, "Looks like I'm not the only person not being honest with Dale. You should tell him."

Changing the subject, Mya said, "Do you know why I stopped eating junk food?"

Shaking her head, Carrie said, "I assume because you learned what it was doing to your system."

"I weighed two hundred and sixty pounds. My nickname growing up was Wide Mya. But as far back as middle school, Dale was the only person who saw *me* and not the fat girl with her nose in a book. He's my friend, and I plan to keep it that way."

Understanding what Mya didn't say, Carrie nodded. "Fair enough. But I hope he gets a clue someday."

"Like you said. He'll find the right girl. Eventually."

"I'll be honest with him after the wedding," she assured her, sliding Molly's diaper bag onto her shoulder.

Mya picked up the giraffe she'd thrown earlier. "Then I'll be ready to help him move on to the next girl."

Carrie's heart went out to her. "Now go stop him from eating another doughnut."

With a resigned smile, Mya left the baby room. On the way to the parking lot, Carrie sent up a little prayer for the stubborn couple.

Chapter 9

The letter stared back at Noah from where he'd thrown it on the table. He should have waited longer to open it.

The dream that had ripped him from sleep at dawn lingered long after he'd washed the sand from his eyes. Most of his nightmares came with a haze around them, as if he watched them through a dirty lens. The sounds were always the worst part. The explosions. The gunfire. The screams. But other than dust and blurry figures, Noah couldn't make out what was going on. Which heightened the fear, because he also couldn't see a way out.

But this morning's dream had been different. Like fucking high-def, he'd seen everything down to the anguish on Deekins's face when the bomb ripped his leg off at mid-thigh. A member of Noah's platoon during his last deployment, the kid had been nineteen years old. He'd enlisted to get away from the gang violence that was pervasive in his neighborhood. Figured if he was going to die at the end of a bullet, he'd do it fighting for his country and not sitting on his porch having a smoke.

Noah had been there when Deekins took the hit. Had fought to slow the bleeding until the medics could reach them, but he hadn't noticed the shrapnel in the boy's neck. Had been too focused on the leg and failed to assess for other injuries. By the time help arrived, the kid was gone.

If only the dream had ended there.

With his hands still covered in blood, Noah found himself standing in the middle of his living room. The room started to spin. Slow, then picking up speed. As he climbed onto the couch, a scream slashed through the silence and the room stopped on a dime, hurling him backward. The scream came again, and Noah ran to the window, but instead of grass and trees he saw nothing but desert. His bloodstained hands created red smudges on the glass when he caught sight of a man dragging Carrie out of a rusted pickup by her hair. He had Molly tucked under his other arm, the child flailing in fear.

"Carrie!" Noah yelled, slamming his hands against the pane.

The frantic mother fought to reach her baby, but the asshole yanked her hair hard enough to send her to her knees.

Noah sprinted to the door, but it wouldn't open. He pounded and kicked as the screams and cries grew louder and louder until his ears threatened to bleed. Shifting back to the window, he yanked with all his strength, but the damn thing wouldn't open. He called her name again, but she couldn't hear him. On her knees, she took a boot kick to the face, and Noah shot out of the dream.

Standing naked in his bathroom, he'd watched drops of water run down his face, feeling as helpless as he had in the dream. This was a new version of hell.

Now, hours later, the memory made him shake with rage. His left leg bounced a steady beat as Noah knocked back half of his soda, never taking his eyes off the letter. He supposed some might consider it good news. He'd been specially selected from an endless supply of defective vets for yet another study. He'd already played the role of guinea pig once, but thanks to the luck of the draw, he'd ended up on the losing team. Or so he assumed. No one shared the details, but he didn't have to be a genius to see that six of the twelve participants had shown marked improvement.

He hadn't been one of the six.

Volunteering to go through another study would be like joining a Russian roulette league. Even if he came through on the winning side, the process would likely leave him more twisted than before. Noah couldn't get his hopes up again. He wouldn't be a number on a page, a statistic in their findings. But what was the alternative? Go back on the meds? Hit the ground every time a car backfired? Flip out on a defenseless woman because she'd tapped him on the shoulder?

Live with nightmares that would drive him mad?

Slamming his elbows on the table, Noah shoved his hands through his hair. Carrie said all he needed was time. What if she was wrong? Patch had put her through enough. She didn't deserve another round of will-he-or-won't-he, and intentional or not, Noah couldn't guarantee that he'd never hurt her.

There was only one option—leave her alone.

Noah wadded the letter into a ball and threw it on the counter. Time to accept that this was how his life would be. Stay busy with work and any project he could find, and steer clear of personal connections. The fewer people in his life the better.

After pulling on his boots, he stepped out the back door on his way to the barn, unable to resist a glance toward Carrie's trailer. She'd pulled out just before nine that morning and had yet to return. Noah didn't know where she'd gone, and he reminded himself that her whereabouts were none of his business.

❧

She'd known by the sound of a roaring engine that Noah had been working in the barn when she and Molly returned from church. Having learned a lesson the hard way, Carrie resisted the urge to pay him a visit. He was working. Enjoyed his projects in the barn. There was no reason she needed to interrupt him.

Except she was dying to see him.

Hours passed until, just before sunset, silence replaced the engine noise. Carrie peeked through the window, which she'd done several times throughout the day, and finally saw Noah trudge back to his house. With the hope that he'd come knocking, she put Molly to bed fifteen minutes earlier than usual. The child drifted off to sleep as the sun gave way to darkness, leaving her mother free for another evening chat on the porch.

Only a knock never came.

He'd likely wanted to shower after working in the barn all day, but that shouldn't have taken this long. In case he was waiting for a sign, Carrie switched on the porch light and stepped outside, staring at the farmhouse as if she could telepathically lure him to her. The only light in the house came from an upstairs window. Maybe he was waiting for her to call, which seemed silly when they were so close, but then men got silly ideas all the time, so Carrie hurried inside for her phone. Back on the porch, she hit Send on the call and watched the window. A shadow danced across the blind a second before the call went to voice mail.

As she lowered the phone from her ear, the light went out, and Carrie's heart dropped. Why didn't he pick up? Why didn't he come over to see her?

What had she done wrong?

Carrie walked back in the house, turned off the porch light, and locked the door. There would be no visitors tonight. Or any night, apparently. Dragging a blanket off the back of the couch, she lay down and reached for the remote. Wilson stretched, then hopped from the coffee table to the couch and curled up on her hip. Eighteen pounds of purring feline was oddly comforting in her current condition.

As she stroked behind the cat's ears, she found an old black-and-white movie that she hadn't seen in forever, but Carrie didn't make it past the first act. Lack of sleep from the night before, and countless nights before that, caught up to her. Somewhere in the middle of the first dance number, she floated off to sleep. Around midnight, she woke to find an infomercial on the television and Wilson snoring on the back of the couch.

Feeling lonelier than she had in a long time, Carrie performed her nightly tasks like a robot. When she reached for the under-eye cream, a depressing thought popped to mind. Why was she bothering? Why did she go through this ritual of moisturizers and beauty creams when she was destined to die an old maid, surrounded by cats and empty TV dinner boxes?

"You're pathetic," she said to her reflection, stopping the pity party right there. "Noah is not the last man on earth, and you are not going to die alone." Dabbing the clear cream under each eye, she created an invisible barrier against future wrinkles, and said, "We will die in the party wing of whatever nursing home Lorelei reserves for us, but when that day comes, Noah Winchester will be nothing more than the fleeting memory of a man who missed his chance."

Pep talk complete, Carrie switched off the bathroom light with an extra swing in her step. If she'd been willing to take a chance on Noah, there was no reason she couldn't take a chance with someone else. Their little session on the glider had reminded her what she was missing, and though Carrie had no intention of humiliating herself on one of those dating sites—something Lorelei had suggested more than once—her man boycott ended now.

◦

"Boss!" yelled Jordan Ethridge, waving his arms in the air.

Noah removed his earplugs. He'd warned all the guys on his crew that if they wanted his attention, they'd have to get in his line of sight, but whatever they did, they were never to touch him.

"What is it?" he asked.

"Are you the person in charge here?" snapped the well-dressed older woman standing next to Jordan.

Without answering, Noah said, "Who are you?"

"I'm Meredith Mitchner, and I'm the chairwoman of the Safe Haven Women's Shelter board. I want to know what's going on here."

As if it wasn't obvious, he said, "We're renovating this old camp to serve as your shelter."

"Amusing, young man." She didn't look amused at all. "We have a December first open date. It's already October. More should be done by now."

"We started the job last week," Noah informed her. "We're working as fast as we can, but we won't cut corners or jeopardize our own safety to hit your deadline."

Bristling, she said, "I don't appreciate your tone."

He didn't give a shit what she appreciated. "And I don't like you showing up on my job site uninvited."

"You listen to me, young man—"

"I'm not your young man. If you have a problem with our work, take it up with Mike Lowry." Noah pushed the earplugs back into place. "We've got work to do."

Noah stepped up to the table saw to cut another two-by-four. Halfway through the wood, his saw shut off. Looking around, he found the intruder holding the plug, one thin eyebrow floating near her hairline.

"What's your problem?" he said, dragging the plugs out of his ears again. "Do you want this job done or not?"

"I want a tour, and I want to know what you've done so far."

"I don't have time to give tours."

"Make time," she ordered.

The hell he would. Noah pulled the cell out of his pocket and dialed Mike's number. The call went to voice mail. He tried again. Straight to the mailbox. He had no choice but to call the last person he wanted to talk to.

"Lowry Construction," Carrie said.

"There's some old woman over here telling me she wants a tour," Noah snarled. "You need to get her out of my way."

"What do you mean an old woman is there?"

Noah pulled the phone from his ear. "What did you say your name is?"

"Meredith Mitchner," she enunciated, as if she were talking to an idiot.

"You hear that?" he said into the phone.

"Oh sweet Jesus," Carrie replied. "I'll be there as quick as I can."

Tucking the phone back into place, he said, "Find a seat outside. Your tour guide will be here in ten minutes."

"What is your name?" she demanded. "I want to make sure Mr. Lowry fires the correct person."

"If Lowry cows to your uppity ass, then I don't want to work for him anyway." Not that Noah could afford to quit, but this would solve the problem of having to deal with Carrie to get his paycheck, which he'd been told to pick up that afternoon.

Avoiding her had been a bitch. During the day, it wasn't so bad since she hadn't paid any visits to the job site. But in the evenings, he had to time his trips to the barn so as not to catch her outside. Deciding he wasn't any good for her was one thing. Being outright rude was another. The weather this week had been more like summer than fall, and mother and daughter had taken advantage of the minor heat wave to spend at least an hour outside each evening.

A couple nights, he would have sworn that she'd stayed out longer on purpose, but then he hadn't lived next to them long enough to know if these nightly playtimes were unusual or not. She hadn't called him since Sunday night when he'd ignored her. Hadn't stopped by or even left a note on his door. Good to know she wasn't losing any sleep over his sudden change of heart.

Noah snatched the cord from the old woman's hand and plugged his saw back in. Before returning to his task, he shot her a warning look that said, *Don't even think about pulling that stunt again.* His adversary marched out of the room, her head high and her ass sashaying all the way. Talk about a ballbuster.

He'd cut five more boards before Jordan waved him down again. "What now?" he growled.

"Carrie asked me to come get you," the young man replied, looking hopeful that Noah wouldn't kill the messenger.

"Where is she?" he asked.

"Down in the center office looking at the plans. That Meredith woman is with her, and she's got questions."

"She can shove her questions up her ass," he mumbled, but Noah stomped down to the office all the same.

"I'm trying to renovate a camp here," he said to the pair he found hunched over the floor plans. "What's your damn question?"

The women met his eye at the same time, but Noah only saw Carrie. The baby-blue top brought out her eyes, and her hair all tucked up on the back of her head like that made him want to trail kisses down her neck. He hadn't expected to have such a powerful reaction to seeing her. His body tightened with need, forcing him to hold his hard hat over his zipper.

"I've assured Meredith that the project will be done by the deadline," Carrie said, avoiding his eyes, "and that our open date will not be delayed, but she's concerned about the pace of the renovations. Could you let her know where we are in the schedule so she feels better about the situation?"

Noah couldn't recite the alphabet, let alone discuss a construction schedule. Not when the blood was rushing from his brain.

"We'll be done," he said. "Interruptions like this don't help." Great. Now she'd turned him into a freaking caveman. Stepping closer to the makeshift desk, he pointed to the right side of the layout. "We're framing in this addition right now." His finger moved to a row of large interior rooms. "Brandon and Jordan are ripping up the floors in these rooms and will start framing out the new bathrooms next week."

"See?" Carrie said. "The shelter is in good hands. Nothing to worry about."

Meredith didn't look convinced. "What about the addition on the other side?" she asked.

"We'll get there," Noah answered. "There shouldn't be any problems if this weather holds out."

"Are you saying that the opening of this shelter is dependent upon the weather?"

"Every construction project is at the mercy of Mother Nature," Carrie said. "There's no way around that. But once these additions reach a certain point, the weather becomes less of a factor."

The pissy one looked to him for confirmation. "She's right," he said. "Now if you'll excuse me."

"Thank you, Noah," Carrie said. "We appreciate you taking the time to talk to us."

"I still plan to discuss your behavior with Mr. Lowry," Meredith drawled. Good for her.

Noah deprived the woman of a response, but made the mistake of locking eyes with Carrie. The truth hit like a punch. She missed him as much as he missed her.

Dammit.

"I've got to go," he said, slamming the hard hat back on his head as he strode from the room.

Chapter 10

"In what prison did Lowry find that man?" Meredith asked.

"Noah wasn't in prison," she said, biting off each word. "He was serving our country in the Middle East. I realize he's a bit gruff, but he's a good man."

"He's rude and obnoxious."

Pot, meet kettle, Carrie thought.

"He's keeping this project moving. The men respect him and have pushed themselves under his leadership. Mike is happy with his results, and so long as the shelter opens on time, we have nothing to complain about."

Meredith hugged her clutch purse to her side. "That young man cursed at me when all I asked for was a tour of the facility."

Knowing the other woman as she did, Carrie said, "Did you *ask* for a tour, or did you demand one?"

Coral lips flattened. "Perhaps you've spent too much time with this Noah person. I don't like your tone."

Don't roll your eyes. Don't roll your eyes.

"*I'm* the construction liaison," Carrie reminded her. "It's my job to make sure this renovation is completed on time and to our satisfaction. It's *your* job to make sure we have the funding in place to operate once the construction is finished. Have I demanded to know what you're doing to ensure that happens?"

"Point made, Ms. Farmer. But the rest of the board has every right to know where we stand."

"And I submit regular updates to the board, as previously discussed."

Carrie maintained her courage in the face of Meredith's evil glare, but it wasn't easy. Haleigh Rae had shared a list of tactics for dealing with her mother when they'd first started this endeavor. Stand your ground. Don't bluff. Do your homework. And never let her see you cry. Lion tamers had it easier than this.

"We need to know immediately if there are any delays."

"Of course," Carrie replied.

Shoulders stiff, Meredith said, "Then I suppose we're finished here."

"Yes, we are."

Halfway to the door, the older woman turned. "Aren't you coming?"

"I have one more thing to do before I go," she said.

Meredith nodded a curt good-bye, leaving Carrie alone in the dusty office. One battle down. One battle to go.

Paychecks in hand, she located the rest of the crew first, saving Noah for last. She'd run through every emotion, from heartbreak and pity to hostility and anger, all in the course of five days, and she'd be damned if she would miss this chance. Noah owed her an explanation. He didn't have to like her. He never had to talk to her again. But today, he would man up and confess what had changed between Saturday night and Sunday afternoon.

When she found him at the saw bench in the addition, he'd just shut down the machine and was wiping the sweat from his brow. His unruly waves had been secured at the back of his neck, and sawdust dotted his beard.

"Hi," she said from the doorway, careful not to startle him.

Noah looked up, clearly surprised to see her. "Hey."

She crossed the space between them. "I brought your paycheck."

"I thought I had to pick it up at the office," he said, wiping dust from the side of the bench. As if the rest of the room weren't covered in the stuff.

"That's how it normally works, but since I had to come to your rescue, I decided to bring them with me."

He shoved the envelope in his back pocket. "I didn't need rescuing."

"Of course not," she agreed, willing to spare his pride. For now. "Are you breaking for lunch?"

"Yep." Still no eye contact.

"Mind if I join you?"

That caught his attention. "I have a bag lunch. There isn't anything to join."

Carrie shrugged, keeping her tone light. "I could sit with you for a while."

"I don't think—"

"Or do you have some sort of communicable disease that I might catch?" she asked, moving closer. "Is that why you stopped coming over? Why you went from 'Give me a chance' to pretending I don't exist? Because if there's nothing wrong with you, then there must be something wrong with me. So which is it, Noah? What am I missing?"

A muscle ticked in his jaw. "Last Saturday was a mistake. I shouldn't have invited you over."

"Really? Why?"

"Why what?"

"Why was it a mistake?"

"It just was." Noah tossed his hard hat into a corner. "I'm saving you a lot of grief. We're both better off this way."

"Don't I get a say?" Carrie rounded the bench, invading his space. Forcing him to look at her. "My whole life men have been making decisions for me. Telling me how to dress and when to speak and to whom, and now you want to tell me what's good for me. When do I get to make some decisions? When do I get to decide what I want and don't want?"

Noah stepped around her toward the exit. "Trust me," he growled, "you don't want this."

He would not walk away from her. Not again. "Give me a reason," Carrie said, hot on his heels. "Why did things change overnight?"

"God, woman, why can't you let this go?"

"Because you're the first man I've wanted anything to do with since Patch died." Noah stopped but didn't turn around. "You're the first man I've even considered letting in, and I don't understand why you don't want me anymore." Tears threatened, but she willed them back.

Running his hands through his hair, Noah shook his head. "It isn't that I don't *want* you, Carrie. It's that I can't *have* you."

"What?" she said, putting herself in front of him. "Noah, that doesn't make any sense. You *can* have me. I'm right here."

"No." The shaking got faster. "It isn't that easy."

Cupping his face in her hands, she made him look at her. "I know that you have challenges. I have challenges, too. I'm afraid of my own shadow. I'm afraid of my own judgment and a million other things, but I'm not afraid of you, Noah. I never thought I would trust anyone again, but I trust you. That has to mean something."

He leaned into her hand. "It means you aren't paying attention. I don't sleep, and when I do, the nightmares are like walking through hell over and over again. I never relax, and I could snap at any time. I won't put you in the line of fire, Carrie. I won't put you back in that place."

"It isn't the same."

"That mark on your throat was the same," he said, trailing a finger where the bruise had been. "When I lose control, I'm not some asshole throwing a backhand to keep his woman in line. I've been trained to do a lot worse than that. You need to get as far away from me as you can."

"And I'm a woman who cheated on her husband after losing his child. A woman who endured abuse and never fought back because somewhere deep inside I believed that I deserved it. I deserved every punch, every kick, because of what I'd done. Neither of us is perfect, Noah, but no matter what you say, I'm not giving up on you."

Brown eyes closed on a heavy sigh. "You don't know what you're signing up for."

Carrie rose on her tiptoes to touch her lips to his. "I want you in my life, Noah. I want to see where this goes."

Pulling her tight against him, he said, "Promise me you'll get out if I lose it. No second chances. If I hurt you again, we're done."

She nodded, willing to say anything to convince him. "I promise."

"God, I've missed you," he said, rubbing a thumb along her jaw.

"How much?" she asked, hoping to tease him into a smile.

"This much," he growled, taking her mouth with his.

The kiss touched all the broken places inside her while igniting the embers that had been smoldering for days. Carrie wrapped herself around him, absorbing his heat and power, giving as much as she took. When his fingers slipped beneath the hem of her shirt, tiny fires danced along her skin.

When Noah broke the kiss, he pressed his forehead against hers while they both caught their breath.

"Does this mean I'll see you tonight?" Carrie asked between pants.

"As soon as I get home," he replied.

Stars once again twinkling overhead, Noah stared at the heavens from Carrie's porch glider as he waited for her to put Molly down to sleep. If someone had told him when he woke that morning that this was where he'd end the day, he'd never have believed them. The doubts were still there. The fear of what might happen. But for now, he would live in the present and enjoy the company of the pretty girl who'd fought to bring him around.

"She's out," Carrie said, joining him on the porch, throwing a blanket over them both once she'd curled up beside him. "All that trike riding wore her out."

Despite his determination to stay away from Carrie, Noah had still taken the time during the week to modify the seat on the ancient tricycle so that Molly could ride it. He'd had to push her around, as her little legs wouldn't reach the pedals for several months, but there was no longer any danger of her falling off.

"I did all the work," Noah reminded her. "My back may never be the same."

"You could have stopped at any time."

"Then she'd have cried."

Carrie flattened her palm over his heart and looked up at him. "She needs to learn the word *no*."

"Not on my watch she doesn't." Noah pulled Carrie tight against him and kissed the top of her head. He'd been waiting for the right time to ask his next question, and hoped he wouldn't upset her. "You said something today about losing a baby. You up for talking about that?"

She laid her cheek against her hand. "His name was Jeremy. The umbilical cord got wrapped around his neck. The doctors weren't able to save him."

Expecting the answer to have been an early-term miscarriage, Noah cursed whatever higher power toyed with people like this. "I'm sorry you had to go through that."

"Me too. Spencer was devastated to lose his son. Neither of us knew how to handle it."

"I can't even imagine what that was like."

She sighed. "It sucked. Big time. That was really the beginning of the end. From that point on, we were like two ghosts living in the same house." Carrie wrapped her arms around his chest. "He shut down, and I blamed myself. My body was supposed to keep the baby alive until he could breathe on his own, but I'd done the opposite. I'd killed him."

Noah pushed her away to look into her eyes. "Honey, you didn't kill anyone. That was a freak thing. If anything, the doctors are the ones to blame. They should have done something. It's their job to make sure shit like that doesn't happen."

"I know *now* that it wasn't my fault. And it wasn't the doctor's fault either," she assured him. "There was nothing they could have done. But back when it happened, it was just too much to process. I think, after that, I was looking for an excuse to make Spencer leave me. That's why I started running around with Patch."

"Why didn't you ask for a divorce?"

"That would have been the adult thing to do." She leaned into him again. "But then it would have felt like Spencer had been the one to do something wrong. Like, me leaving him would be adding insult to injury, if that makes any sense."

In some twisted way, her logic made perfect sense. Especially knowing her state of mind at the time.

"You felt like a bad person, so you did something that would make him see you as a bad person."

Her head tilted. "That's it exactly. The divorce was the punishment for losing the baby, but then the abuse started, and it was the punishment for being unfaithful." Voice brittle, she said, "I swear, I can rationalize anything."

A habit that ignited concern in Noah. He lifted her onto his lap. "You do not deserve to be punished for anything. Do you hear me? No one should ever touch you in anger. Ever. Tell me you believe that."

"Noah, you aren't going to hurt me."

"Dammit, Carrie, this is important. Say it. No one gets to hurt you. No one."

Gripping his hand, she held it to her chest. "I told you before. I made myself a vow that I'd never let anyone hurt me again. And I won't." With a kiss on his knuckles, she said, "Now what about you?"

"Someone hurting me isn't the problem."

She shook her head. "You are not defective or broken, Noah. You're a good man who deserves to be happy. I want you to believe that."

"I can't believe a lie," he said.

"Do you see me as damaged?" Carrie asked.

Brushing her hair out of her eyes, he said, "I see you as perfect."

"I am far from perfect. I have scars. Inside and out. But hearing you say that gives me hope that I can get there. We can both get there, Noah."

Noah wanted to believe that was true, but he couldn't ignore reality. "How about if for now, you believe enough for the both of us?"

Sliding her hands into his hair, she nodded, bumping her nose against his. "I can do that." With a smile in her voice, she said, "What do you say we stop talking and pick up where we left off this afternoon?"

Noah nibbled her bottom lip. "I'm starting to think you like me."

"You think?" she asked, laughter drifting into a purr as his fingers trailed up her back. "I hope you're prepared for something more than kissing on this porch."

His hands stopped. "Shit."

Carrie dropped her head onto his shoulder. "That is not the answer I was hoping for."

Wanting more than anything to please the woman in his arms, Noah shifted her onto the bench seat, cradling her back with his arm while his other hand reached for the button on her jeans. "There are other things we can do."

"I thought you said—"

"Shh, honey. Let me take care of you."

"Oh," Carrie whispered, followed by a deep sigh when his fingers dipped into her panties. "Oh boy."

He kissed her chin before trailing his tongue down the side of her neck to the exposed skin above the top button of her shirt. "Is that good?" he asked, exploring deeper until his fingers found her wet and ready.

"Good," she breathed. "So good."

His mouth closed over her breast, biting through the shirt and bra at the same time he pressed a circle over her clit. Carrie gripped his arm as she panted his name. "Noah, I can't hold on. It's too much."

"Let it go, baby. Let me do this for you."

Her legs spread wider, allowing him more access. He entered her with one finger, nice and slow, and then another.

Carrie bucked against him. "Don't stop. Please don't stop."

"Never, baby."

His dick pressed so hard against his jeans Noah feared permanent damage. But this was her night. He could get his own later.

Withdrawing, he pressed deeper. Harder. His thumb hit her clit, and Carrie burst apart in his arms, his name on her lips as she rode him through it. Noah held her close as she found her way back to earth, breathing heavily as the tremors faded until she was languid against him.

When she finally opened her eyes, Noah hovered above her. "How was that?"

"Better than I remember," she murmured. "I may never be able to move again."

Noah chuckled. "This glider is my new favorite spot, but a lifetime on here wouldn't be all that comfortable."

"Give me a minute," she said, waving a hand in the air. "I think my brain is returning to solid form." Leaning up on her elbows, she blew a hair out of her eyes. "You're good at that."

He wiggled a brow. "You should see what else I can do."

"Don't toy with me when you aren't prepared for an immediate demonstration."

She had a point. Noah lifted her into a sitting position on the seat next to him. "I'd better get back to my side of the fence."

"But you didn't—"

A kiss cut off her words. "We'll take care of me the next time. What are you doing tomorrow night?"

"I don't know," she said, her head dropping onto the back of the glider. "What day is it?"

"Tomorrow is Saturday," he informed her.

"Dang." Carrie threw an arm over her eyes. "The bachelorette party."

Hiding his disappointment, he said, "So we wait until Sunday."

"Waiting sucks," she grumbled. "And you didn't—"

"If you start talking dirty, I won't be going anywhere. Prepared or not." Noah rose to his feet, pulling her with him.

Carrie slid her arms around his neck. "So dirty talk turns you on, huh?"

Showing her exactly how turned on he was, he said, "*You* turn me on. The dirty talk would be a bonus."

Revealing an unexpected seductive side, she said, "I'll remember that." His dick twitched. "Well, hello there," she hummed, grinding against him.

"Now you really are trying to kill me." Noah put as much distance between them as he could while keeping his lips locked on hers.

Breaking the connection, he groaned. "Have fun at your party. And no fondling the strippers."

Pulling the blanket off the glider, she said, "No promises."

Trudging through the gate, Noah pointed her way. "You want to fondle someone, you fondle me."

"I'm trying," she said with a laugh.

"Sunday," he barked.

"Sunday," she replied.

Chapter 11

Lorelei had no idea the sacrifice Carrie was making. Her body had been buzzing like a live wire all day, and she would much rather be throwing sparks with Noah than celebrating the end of her friend's single-hood. It wasn't as if Lorelei would lament giving up her freedom. She was the happiest bride Carrie had ever seen, and she and Spencer had been waiting for this day for more than thirteen years.

"I still don't understand why you had to come and get us instead of Cooper," she said, standing on the running board to lift Molly from the backseat of Spencer's truck. "His house is closer, and you shouldn't have had to go out of your way."

Spencer joined Carrie on the passenger side and took Molly so she could climb down. Champ barreled around the truck to welcome his owner and slobber all over Molly's shoe. The baby giggled as the black Lab licked her hand.

"Give us some room, buddy," Spencer said. "Cooper had something else he needed to do."

"Since when?" she asked. "It's bad enough that you guys wouldn't let any of us drive. What are you up to?"

In an odd plot twist, Spencer, Snow's husband, Caleb, and Cooper had taken over the planning of Lorelei's bachelorette party, and then they'd insisted on keeping the details a secret. Carrie, Snow, Haleigh, and Cooper's sister Abby were all to receive rides to the Pratchett house, which seemed to be the launching point for the festivities. The logistics worked well for Carrie since Lorelei's grandmother, Rosie Pratchett, would be keeping Molly for the night, but that didn't mean she liked being kept in the dark.

"You'll see," he replied, relieving Carrie of the diaper bag and trudging across the yard. "Look what I found, Rosie."

"There's my little angel," the older woman crowed, waiting on the porch with open arms. Molly recognized one of her primary spoilers immediately and dove for her. Rosie kissed the baby's cheek. "You get bigger every time I see you."

"It's only been a week," Carrie reminded the older woman.

"But a week is like months when they're this young."

She couldn't argue with that, having just last night shown Noah some pictures from the week Molly had been born. Carrie still couldn't believe she'd ever been that tiny.

Champ broke into a barking fit as a white Jeep pulled up the drive and the rest of the party spilled onto the grass. Caleb opened his wife's door and held her hand as if they were high school sweethearts. They really were annoyingly adorable together.

"Do we know where we're going yet?" Haleigh Rae asked.

"I'm still in the dark," Carrie said. "Rosie, where's Lorelei?"

"She's putting together some last-minute items for the party."

"So she knows what's going on?" Abby asked.

"Nope," Spencer said. "She's as clueless as the rest of you." He smiled like the conniving charmer he was. "Patience, ladies."

"Why did we agree to this?" Snow asked.

Caleb kissed her knuckles. "Because we didn't give you a choice."

The screen door slammed behind them, drawing everyone's attention. "Let's get this show on the road," Lorelei hollered, stopping when she caught sight of Molly. "How is my sweet cuddle bug today? Are you ready for a fun night with Granny?" Molly responded to the kiss on her nose by yanking Lorelei's hair. "Girly, I cannot wait until you stop doing that."

"What's in those?" Snow asked, pointing to the colorful gift bags dangling from Lorelei's arm.

"Bachelorette party accessories, of course."

Carrie didn't like the sound of that. "Don't make us wear something weird."

"It's my party and I'll do weird if I want to." The bride-to-be handed each woman a bag. "Besides, these aren't weird. They're fun."

The guests reached into the tissue paper with little enthusiasm.

"No way," Haleigh murmured as Carrie spotted the purple feathers in her bag.

Abby pulled a pink boa from hers. "You don't really expect us to wear these."

"I don't know," Snow said, wrapping a royal-blue one around her neck. "I like it."

"We'll look like showgirls," Haleigh argued.

"No one better lose enough clothes to qualify as a showgirl," Caleb warned. "And it looks like your ride is here."

Brushing feathers away from her face, Carrie looked down the driveway to see a black SUV limo coming their way.

"Get out," Lorelei said, smacking Spencer on the arm. "That's for us?"

"Our girls go in style," he answered.

As the limo drew closer, Haleigh said, "That better not be who I think it is behind the wheel."

"We wanted to make sure you ladies were well taken care of."

"You put a spy in the car," Abby corrected.

The vehicle parked behind Spencer's truck, and Cooper stepped out. Removing his telltale ball cap, he bowed. "Your chariot has arrived."

Lorelei and Snow attempted to peek through the tinted windows while Haleigh said, "And where is our chariot driver?"

"You're looking at him." Before his girlfriend could argue, Cooper swept her into a long, hard kiss. "Consider me driver and moral support."

Though not common knowledge around town, the friends gathered were aware of Haleigh's battle with alcohol addiction. She'd sworn that the others drinking during the party wouldn't bother her, but Carrie could see relief in her eyes at the idea of Cooper being close by while she faced down temptation.

Ruffling the curls along his collar, the blonde said, "You *are* cute." Turning to the ladies, she added, "No one tell my boyfriend that I hooked up with the driver, okay?"

The gang agreed to keep her secret as Cooper laughed into Haleigh's hair.

"What are we waiting for?" Lorelei said. "Let's check this thing out."

The mechanic turned chauffeur opened the back door to let his passengers crawl inside. By the time Carrie's butt hit the seat, Lorelei had already popped the cork on the bottle of champagne.

"Hal," Cooper whispered. "Check the minifridge."

The doctor followed the suggestion to find the bottom of the fridge stocked with soda and water. Carrie smiled at the extra effort he'd gone to. She'd witnessed Haleigh's tumble off the wagon back in the spring, and it had not been pretty. She also knew that Cooper had loved Haleigh for years before the workaholic doc had finally opened her eyes to what she was missing. Maybe that's what had prompted Carrie's change of heart in the dating department. Spending the majority of her time with three gag-inducing happy couples had renewed her faith in love. Or at least shown her that happy endings really were possible.

Lorelei shoved a glass of bubbly into Carrie's hand and raised her own. "To my last girls' night out as a single lady. Let's make it a good one."

"Hear, hear!" they chimed in unison, glasses tinkling together with one non-tinkling plastic bottle.

Once the glasses had been tipped, Lorelei filled them again. "So where are we going?" Abby asked. They all exchanged blank stares. Cooper had already closed the door and taken his place in the driver's seat, but the glass divider prevented them from asking. The SUV started rolling backward, nearly sending them all onto the floor.

"I guess we'll find out when we get there," Snow said, bracing herself against the back of the seat.

By the time they'd reached the main road, Lorelei had popped a second bottle of champagne, which explained the hum in Carrie's ears. She couldn't remember the last time she'd had this much to drink. At the rate this party was going, they'd have to peel her off the seat to get her home.

Despite the fact that his body ached as if he'd done a drop without his parachute, Noah wouldn't trade the night before for anything. Carrie's unwavering belief that they could defeat, or at least subdue, the demon in his brain offered the one thing he'd forsaken—hope. Like a black cloud shielding a deadly tornado, his future had loomed in the distance waiting to tear him apart. It wasn't a matter of *if* he lost it, but *when*.

Until Carrie walked into his life.

A memory sprang to mind. An encounter Noah hadn't thought about in nearly a year. With the glare of a drill sergeant, a hard-ass doctor had shut down his pity party. According to Doc Levine, contrary to everything Noah believed about his situation, his brain *could* recover. It wouldn't be easy, and he might never get back to where he'd been before his first deployment, but the one way to guarantee a permanent place in the abyss was to give up. To admit defeat and let the disorder run amok.

That had been the day he'd joined the first study, confident that things would change. Six months later, the study ended, and nothing had changed. Not for him. But others had seen improvement. Or so he'd believed, until a couple of months later when he'd spotted a familiar name in an online article. William Lewis had been one of the lucky six in Noah's study who'd come out the other side a new man. Except the effects hadn't lasted. The soldier had put a gun in his mouth and shut off the noise for good.

No way would Noah become a statistic. Regardless of the nightmares and the headaches and the constant fear, there would be no early exit for him. At least not at his own hand. Which was why he refused to keep a gun in the house. No guns. No alcohol. No desperate acts of stupidity or desperation. This defect might steal his nights, but it wouldn't take his life.

Especially not now.

After leaving Carrie on her porch, he'd jumped in a lukewarm shower, given his body the release it needed, and settled on the couch with the latest copy of *Cycle World* magazine. Around midnight, he'd snagged the open bag of chips from the pantry and switched over to *American Iron*, but before long, he'd drifted off to sleep with the lights still on. When he woke, the sun hung high in the sky, and though he'd dreamed about being back in the desert, none of the usual scenes had played out. No explosions. No carnage. No nightmares.

A full night's sleep was rare, and Noah hadn't felt this awake in longer than he could remember. Focusing on the chores in the house first, he finished two loads of laundry, washed the dishes that had been piling up since the weekend before, and kept a constant eye on Carrie's trailer. When the Dodge Ram had pulled into her drive, he'd fought the urge to step outside.

While the stranger buckled Molly into the backseat of his truck, Carrie glanced over to the farmhouse three or four times. He assumed she hoped he wasn't watching to see her drive off with another man, but then the truck pulled out of the drive and he spotted the words **BOYD'S CUSTOM CABINETS** displayed across the tailgate. Several seconds later, Noah realized why the name sounded familiar.

Carrie's last name had been Boyd when Noah met her. Which meant her escort had been her ex-husband and the future groom. Guilt churned in his gut for assuming that Carrie had been sneaking off with someone else. As if having the guy pull into her driveway in the light of day was the way to keep him a secret.

Two hours later, Noah was still kicking himself for not going out to say good-bye when he heard the knock. Due to the warm weather, he'd left the inside door open and spotted Kyra through the screen. Well, hell.

"What's going on?" he said.

"And howdy-do to you, hot stuff. I thought I'd come out and check on you."

"I don't need to be checked on."

"Aw, come on, Noah. I've got one of Mama's pecan pies." She held a brown bag in the air. "Let me in."

Against his better judgment, Noah unhooked the latch on the door. "For a minute," he said, holding it open.

Kyra's breasts brushed his chest as she entered. The sleeveless flannel tied at her waist hung open wide enough to reveal the lace along the top of her bra. From his vantage point, Noah could see a lot more than lace.

"Is the kitchen back here?" she asked, continuing through the living room without waiting for a response.

"You can put the pie in the fridge," he said when he caught up to her.

"Don't be silly." Kyra pulled the pie and a tub of whipped cream out of the bag before moving to the cupboards. Noah remained in the doorway to the living room, watching her carry plates and silverware to the table. "You don't even have a clock on the wall," she said, lifting the foil off the pie. "This place needs a woman's touch. I'll have to hit up some of the flea markets in town and see what I can find for you."

"I like it the way it is." Noah crossed his arms over his chest. "Why are you here, Kyra?"

She dished two slices onto the plates and reached for the whipped topping. "Stop acting like a grumpy bear and come over here. We both know you're dying for a piece of this pie." Red lips curled into a seductive smile. "I brought it just for you," she purred, licking cream off her finger.

Noah nearly rolled his eyes. "I told you before, Kyra, I'm not interested in what you're offering."

"But you love Mama's pecan pie."

"This isn't a game. Go home to your husband."

Undeterred, she twirled a lock of black hair around her finger as she strutted toward him. "Lenny's boring. That's why we have our arrangement. He gets to show me off to his friends at those dumb dinner parties, and I get to amuse myself elsewhere."

"I'm not here for your amusement," Noah said. "And you're better than this sex kitten act."

Green eyes snapped with anger. "I've got boys all over town itching to spend time with me."

"I'm not a *boy*." He nodded toward the table. "Pack up and go home."

Jaw tight, she marched to the table and slammed the food back in the bag. "You always were an arrogant bastard."

"And you were a good kid. What happened, Kyra?"

"Shove it, Noah." Stomping past him, she slammed through the screen door. As he stepped onto the porch, he witnessed the pie fly through the open window of a burgundy Camaro, but instead of getting in the car, Kyra stepped through the gate toward Carrie's trailer.

"What are you doing?" he yelled.

"None of your business," she hurled back, flipping him the middle finger over her head.

Before he reached the edge of the yard, she was pounding on Carrie's front door.

"She isn't home," he said. "You're wasting your time."

Throwing her hands on her hips, Kyra said, "So you know her comings and goings now? What, do you watch her through your little window like some nosy old lady?"

Tired of dealing with the petulant child, Noah ignored the question and ambled back to his porch.

"Are you friends with this bitch?" she demanded, returning to his property.

Noah spun. "Don't call her a bitch."

Kyra stared openmouthed. "You can't be serious. You're fucking my brother's slut?"

"Watch your mouth," he growled.

"I can't believe you'd take her over me."

"I'm not taking anyone. Go home, Kyra."

Shaking her head, she fumed. "She's the reason he's dead. Did you know that?"

"What are you talking about?"

"No matter what he gave her, she was never happy. She acted like she couldn't stand for him to touch her. Made him feel worthless, and that's why he got drunk that night. That's why he got in that fight. Because those assholes were taunting him about his tail-swishing wife." Kyra snarled, "He died defending her, and she didn't even deserve it."

"Enough," Noah roared. "Get out of here. Now."

Backing toward her car, Kyra said, "You'll regret getting mixed up with her." The Camaro rumbled to life and sent gravel flying when she stomped on the gas, sending the car hurdling into the road.

Chapter 12

Who knew that Abigail Williams would be a horny drunk?

"It's been so long," Abby said, waving her champagne glass in the air, "I think I have tumbleweeds rolling around in there."

Carrie patted her on the arm. "But I bet they're pretty tumbleweeds."

The tipsy widows had paired off toward the front of the limo, while the chicks getting regular sex giggled in the back. Slouched low in the seat, they consoled each other on their crappy luck and nonexistent bedroom activities. Abby had lost her husband to a roadside bomb in Afghanistan the year before. Which reminded Carrie how lucky Noah was to have survived that war. And that her brother had been on a sub out of harm's way.

"Kyle was good, you know? I mean. Well. Most of the time." In a stage whisper, she said, "I had to fake it now and then, but who hasn't?"

"Amen, sister." They attempted a high five, but missed. "Patch was selfish. If you know what I mean."

"Oh, that's the worst." After two tries, Abby sat up. "What is wrong with men? We're attractive, smart, sexually adventurous women." Carrie wasn't so sure about that last part, but she didn't interrupt. "We're young. We've still got plenty of good years in us."

"Yes, we do," Carrie agreed, saluting with her glass. "Preach it, girlfriend."

"What are we preaching?" Haleigh asked, reaching into the fridge for a soda.

"That men should be trying to have sex with us."

"Well, okay then." Haleigh turned toward Lorelei and Snow. "Abbs is talking sex. Y'all need to get up here."

"On our way." Lorelei dragged Snow the length of the limo, and they both plopped down on the seat across from the fridge. "We're here. Continue."

"Carrie and I need to find guys to have sex with," Abby said.

"Wait," Carrie said, sitting up straight, "I didn't—"

"Are we talking boyfriend material or a one-night stand?" Lorelei asked, as if they were hashing out a fast-food order. "Because we need to tell Cooper whether to head for Brubaker's or hit the interstate toward Silverado."

She'd heard of the dance hall in Goodlettsville, but Carrie had never been.

"We're talking serious drought here," Abby said before finishing her drink. "One night isn't going to be nearly enough."

"Brubaker's it is." Lorelei knocked on the divider between them and their driver. When the window lowered, she said, "Take us to Brubaker's, Coop. We have women on a mission back here."

"Yes, ma'am," he said, and the window rose back into place.

"I'm not on a mission," Carrie said, letting Haleigh refill her glass. "I don't want to pick up a guy at a bar."

"So dance and have a little fun," Snow said. "And let a guy pick you up."

"But I don't need to be picked up," she argued.

"Did you finally put batteries in that Rabbit I bought you?" Lorelei asked. "It's about damn time."

Carrie rolled her eyes.

"I thought about buying my mom one of those," Haleigh mumbled. "She'd freak out, but I bet her mood would improve within a week."

And now she was imagining Meredith with a sex toy and might never be able to look the woman in the eye again.

"What kind of rabbit are you guys talking about?" asked Abby.

Haleigh patted her best friend on the knee. "I'll explain later, hon."

"You still need to find a man," Lorelei said.

"No I don't," Carrie argued.

"Why not? If you'd just—"

Frustrated with the conversation, Carrie snapped, "I don't need to find a man because I have Noah."

All eyes locked on Carrie as Abby said, "Does she mean she named a sex toy Noah?"

"You're screwing your neighbor?" Lorelei asked.

"Go, Carrie," Haleigh cheered.

Feeling the heat spread up her neck, Carrie wished the words back into her mouth. This was the champagne's fault. Damn those tasty bubbles.

"I haven't had sex with Noah," she explained. "I mean, I don't think last night counts as having sex."

"What happened last night?" Snow asked.

Abby piped up before Carrie could answer. "You're worse off than me if you don't even know what qualifies as sex."

Great. Maybe she could throw herself out of the car. A little road burn would be less humiliating than this conversation.

"Well?" Haleigh said. "You can't leave us hanging. What happened?"

Before replying, Carrie drank her champagne like a shot and wiped her mouth on her sleeve. The bubbles went straight to her head, which was already floating.

"We've been spending the evenings after Molly goes to sleep talking on my porch."

"Talking?" Haleigh said.

"It starts out as talking. And then kissing . . ."

"You are the slowest storyteller ever," Lorelei whined.

Cutting to the point, Carrie blurted, "We haven't had sex because neither one of us is prepared."

The car went silent.

"Either I'm really drunk or she's talking in riddles," Abby said.

Lorelei shushed her. "Prepared how?"

Mortified, Carrie whispered, "Condoms."

"*That's* the only thing keeping you from jumping this man's bones?"

"I still want to know what didn't qualify as sex," Haleigh said.

Carrie squirmed in her seat. "Since we weren't . . . prepared," she said, "Noah took care of me."

"He took care of . . ." Abby started.

"He gave her an orgasm, Abbs," Haleigh clarified.

"Oh," she answered. "I miss those."

Snow burst out laughing as Lorelei pounded on the glass divider again. "Cooper, we have a change of plans!"

Cooper cleared his throat as the window dropped. "Where to."

"Puckett's Pharmacy."

"Good idea," he replied as the window shot back up.

Haleigh glanced at Lorelei. "That divider thing is soundproof, right?"

"Of course." Tipping the bottle in her hand, the bride poured the last of its contents into her glass. "Looks like we need another bottle. Carrie is getting laid tonight, and that deserves a toast."

"Wait. What?" Carrie said as Abby popped the cork on bottle number three.

"If I'm the only one going home alone," the other widow said, "I might as well keep drinking."

"Don't give up hope yet," Lorelei said. "We'll head to the bar after dropping off Carrie."

What the heck? "You're kicking me out of the party?" she said.

Lorelei passed the champagne from Abby to Snow. "We're taking you home to have your own party. Armed with a full box of condoms."

It might have been the bubbly talking, but Carrie liked the sound of that.

"What am I supposed to do? Knock on his door and say, 'We're having sex'?"

"Or just jump him," Snow said. "He'll get the message."

"I don't know if I can do that," she said, sitting back and sipping her drink. "What if he doesn't want to?"

Four women exchanged telling looks and in unison said, "He'll want to."

When the limo stopped in front of Puckett's Pharmacy, Carrie was too drunk to notice they'd stopped moving. Which was good, because she never could have endured the scene inside the store when her fellow partiers debated Noah's size—loudly and with hand gestures—if she'd been sober.

∽

Noah took a break from working in the barn to grab a bite to eat. Per the usual, the fridge offered little, and the cupboards were nearly bare. He almost wished Kyra had left him the damn pie. Althea made a mean pecan pie. He settled for a nearly empty bag of chips, standing with his back to the sink to eat them. Three handfuls in, he heard loud music in

Terri Osburn

the distance. Leaving the bag on the counter, he stomped to the front door, expecting to find a carload of teenagers disturbing his peace.

He had not expected to see a black SUV limo with a woman sticking out of the top, red feathers flapping around her neck and arms wide in the air. "We come prepared!" she yelled, which made no sense at all.

The limo parked behind his truck, kicking on the motion floodlight on the corner of the house. As soon as the guy stepped out of the car, Noah recognized the driver as the one in the picture with Molly on his shoulders. Cooper opened one of the back doors, and Carrie all but fell into the dirt. Thankfully, the big guy caught her, lifted her onto her feet, and held on until she appeared steady enough to walk.

Covering his mouth to hide the smirk, Noah leaned against a porch post and watched her careen in his general direction. Three more women popped up through the sunroof, all sporting colorful feathers and cheering his drunk little neighbor onward.

"Go get him, girlfriend!"

"You've got this, Carrie!"

"You guys are embarrassing her."

"Good gravy, where can I find one of those?"

Noah took the last as a compliment, though he had no idea which lady to thank. When Carrie reached the bottom step, she grabbed the railing to steady herself, clinging tightly to a brown paper bag in her other hand. After a couple of deep breaths, she gave the limo crew a thumbs-up and then did the last thing he expected.

Charging up the steps, she flung herself at him, wrapping her legs around his waist at the same time her mouth closed over his. Two seconds after the attack, Noah recovered from the shock and crushed her to him. The cheering continued as the limo backed out of the drive, but he was too busy tasting the sweet champagne on her lips to notice.

118

Still clinging to his neck, Carrie broke the kiss, her breath coming in quick pants and her eyes darkened to a cobalt blue. "I'm prepared this time. I don't want to wait until tomorrow, Noah. Let's have sex. Please."

The trepidation in her voice nearly undid him. At a loss for words, he let his actions do the talking.

Pressing her back to the post, Noah cradled her ass while his tongue tangled with hers. He ground against her core, dragging a moan from deep in her chest.

"I need you, Noah," she begged. "I need you so bad."

Aroused to the point of pain, Noah carried her into the house, kicking the door shut behind him. They tasted and nibbled all the way up the stairs, stopping at the top, where he pressed her to the wall and tasted the heat at the base of her neck. He licked his way to her ear and bit the lobe.

"Clothes," she panted. "Too many clothes."

Holding her up with his hips, Noah tugged his T-shirt over his head. Her fingers went straight to the hair on his chest, finding the scar behind the fur.

"How did you get this?"

"Not important," he said, preferring not to discuss his battle wounds. "You said something about being prepared?"

Biting her bottom lip, Carrie nodded. "We stopped for a box of condoms on the way here."

Thank God. "Remind me to thank your friends later."

Trailing a finger down the middle of his chest, she purred, "This *was* their idea. We need to send them something nice."

"I'll get right on that," he said, taking her mouth again.

Seconds later they reached his bed, mostly by luck, since he was too busy savoring the woman in his arms to watch where he was going. Noah let her slide down his body, lifting the hem of her shirt as she went. The feathered scarf came off with the shirt, and both flew through the air as his lips closed over gauzy lace. Carrie shoved her hands into his hair as her body bowed for him.

Teasing her nipple through the material, Noah undid the hooks in the back with one hand and dragged delicate straps off her shoulders. The brown bag landed on the bed as she sighed against him. Cupping her breasts, he stared into her eyes, seeing his own desire reflected in their blue depths.

"I'll never be worthy of this," he confessed.

"Shhh," she murmured, brushing her fingers over his lips. "None of that tonight."

Kissing the tip of her finger, he brushed his thumbs over her nipples. When she moaned, he said, "I want to make you do that all night long."

Pressing against his hands, she reached for the button on his jeans. "I want that, too. But I have a favor to return first, remember?" Carrie bit his nipple at the same time she lowered his zipper. When her fingers touched his cock, Noah surrendered to the fire.

Carrie licked her way down Noah's hard body, sampling every dip and groove as she went. The moment she pushed cotton and denim over his incredible backside, he sprang free, red and pulsing and all for her.

She blew over the tip, eliciting a guttural moan from his broad chest. Carrie couldn't remember ever feeling this powerful. Noah didn't even attempt to take control. To set the pace. No demands or criticism. Only total surrender. His hand in her hair gentle. Patient but desperate for more. The first taste was hot and salty, and Noah's body shook with need. Determined to give as much as he had, she took him deep, gripping his thighs, marveling at the ripple of muscle as he fought to stay upright.

"Carrie, baby. That's so good."

Scraping her nails down the back of his legs, she sucked harder, emboldened by his sighs of pleasure. She remembered how it had felt when he touched her, and her own arousal grew. Increasing the pace, Carrie cupped his balls, and Noah growled as his hips thrust forward.

"I'm on the edge, honey. Your hot little mouth is driving me crazy."

He thrust harder with every suck until his body went stiff and the warm liquid hit the back of her throat. She held on through the tremors, licking the last drop from his tip before Noah lifted her onto the bed and tumbled down beside her. His body continued to shake while he buried his face in her neck.

"Not a bad start?" she said, hoping he didn't plan on taking a nap before they got to the good stuff.

Noah flipped onto his back. "Best start ever."

Encouraging words, but his eyes were still closed. Seconds passed as she waited for him to make a move. The clock ticked. Her buzz faded.

"If you're tired, I should go," she said, rising off the bed.

"Oh no you don't," he said, pulling her on top of him until they were chest to chest, his penis twitching against her stomach. "Now why would you want to leave after that?"

She twirled her finger in his chest hair. "You looked ready to fall asleep."

"Honey," he said, wedging an arm behind his head, "I'm a thirty-four-year-old man who hasn't had sex in nearly a year. You're lucky I lasted as long as I did, but you're going to have to give me a second to recover."

Carrie wasn't accustomed to this kind of honesty. "I assumed you were done. For the night."

His laughter forced her to hold on to his shoulders. "Darling, we could spend a week in this bed and I still wouldn't be done with you." Without warning, he rolled until they'd switched positions. "Now, I think it's time we get you out of those jeans and open the present you brought." Warm lips brushed her collarbone. "Isn't that what you want, honey?" A wet tongue circled her left nipple. "For me to taste you. To be inside you, buried deep when the orgasm hits, making you melt all over me."

Sweet Jesus, he was good at this.

He took her breast in his mouth, stealing her ability to think let alone speak. All Carrie could do was feel. His mouth. His heat. His rock-hard ass. And something else that proved recovery time was over.

Noah lifted himself off the bed, standing before her with no shame or reserve, a man well aware of his power and prowess. His eyes devoured her, intensifying the heat between her legs.

"The jeans?" he said, one heavy brow lifted. She'd assumed he intended to remove them, but Noah showed no signs of reaching for her. Holding his gaze, she unbuttoned the pants and lifted her bottom to shimmy them down her legs. He finally offered assistance when the denim reached her ankles. Without breaking eye contact, he tugged the jeans over her feet and threw them on the floor. "I'll take it from here," he said, placing one knee on the bed.

To her surprise, he reached over her and flicked on the bedside lamp. "What are you doing?"

"I want to see you while we do this. Watch your eyes darken when I touch you." Following words with action, he pressed one finger against her panties. "Like that."

He could watch anything he wanted so long as he kept touching her there.

"You like that?" he asked, rubbing against her clit.

"Yes," she cried. "Do it again." Noah honored her command, this time sliding her panties to the side to put skin on skin. "That's it." Her hips rose off the bed. "More, Noah. Please. I need more."

The panties followed the rest of her clothes to the floor before he lifted her knees to plant her feet on the bed. "Time to prepare," he said, his voice deep and full of promise. He ripped the box of condoms open and tore through a package with his teeth. Watching him slide the thin barrier over his erection was the most erotic thing Carrie had ever witnessed. When he was completely sheathed, Noah took his position between her legs, lifting one of her ankles to rest on his shoulder. "Scoot down for me, baby."

Anticipation beat a steady rhythm through her bloodstream as heat pooled between her legs. True to his word, he watched her face as he slid two fingers inside her. Carrie fisted her hands in the blanket as her back arched.

"So wet, baby."

In one swift motion, he removed his fingers and lifted her hips to drive inside. Every fiber of her being cried out in pleasure. This was what she wanted. What she needed. Noah withdrew and entered again with slow but deliberate movements. Each thrust driving her higher. Fanning the flame she feared might consume her.

"I can't hold back anymore," he growled, dropping her foot to the bed and leaning over her as he thrust in harder.

"Don't hold back," she said, locking her hands around his neck. "This is what I want, Noah. You're what I want."

Everything shifted into high gear as he doubled the pace. Carrie held on, heat coiling through her body as muscles tensed and toes dug into the bed. When he reached down to cup her bottom, lifting her at an angle as he plunged deep, her tether snapped and the world fell away, replaced by light and wave after wave of wicked sensations that numbed her teeth and overwhelmed her mind. The echo of his name still rang in her ears when she opened her eyes to see Noah hovering above her, teeth bared and eyes closed tight. With one final thrust, he roared his release before dropping his forehead to her chest.

Shaking, content, and happier than she'd ever been, Carrie brushed damp strands off his forehead as the last of the orgasm rippled through him. Muscles like hot steel slowly relaxed until he collapsed atop her. Neither spoke as she traced the tattoo on his shoulder. She'd seen the image before but never on someone's skin. A helmet balanced on the handle of a weapon held upright by a pair of boots.

"For the friends I lost," he said quietly against her neck.

Carrie nodded, emotion clogging her throat. He'd been through so much. Too much. And yet he was still gentle and generous and caring. The kind of man a woman would be lucky to have in her life. The kind of man she would fight to *keep* in her life.

Chapter 13

The first thing Noah realized as he drifted awake on that bright Sunday morning was the woman snoring softly near his chin. Eyes still closed, he smiled. But a second revelation followed the first as he registered the soreness in his thighs and lower back. A reminder that he'd been away from the gym for far too long. The third revelation hit the strongest.

No nightmares. No dreams at all. Granted, they'd probably slept maybe five or six hours, but that was a non-nightmare record in his world.

Careful not to jostle the woman sprawled across his chest, Noah checked the clock beside the bed. Nine thirty. Another record. He hadn't slept past O-seven-hundred since before boot camp. As he extended one leg, Carrie curled up tighter along his side, causing a reaction that was evident through the sheet.

"Why is it so bright in here?" she asked, tossing a leg over his hip.

"I don't have curtains," he answered, formulating a plan for how they could spend the morning.

Carrie lifted her head to rest her chin on his sternum. "How do you not have curtains?" She perused the room and said, "You don't have anything. Noah, where's all your furniture?"

"If you haven't noticed, you're on a bed," he said. "That's all I need in here."

Leaning up higher, she checked the walls behind her, providing a mouthwatering view of pink-tipped breasts. "You don't even have a nightstand."

Noah pointed to his left. "I have a stool. It works." The short, round wooden barstool fit the clock and a lamp. And his Louis L'Amour paperback.

Blue eyes went wide. "Nine thirty?" she exclaimed, hopping off the bed. "I was supposed to pick up Molly by nine. Our service has already started, and Rosie's church starts in half an hour." Scrambling to find her clothes, she shot him a frustrated look. "Could you not have thrown them all in the same spot? Where's my bra?"

"Calm down, hon." Noah preferred the purring woman he'd spent the night with to this morning version. Sitting on the edge of the bed, he spotted her bra hanging from the empty curtain rod over the window. "If your church stuff has already started, then you won't make it anyway. And whoever Rosie is, I'm sure she won't mind taking Molly with her."

"I need to call her." She searched the pockets of her jeans. "Where's my phone?"

He snatched the bra off the curtain rod. "I haven't seen a phone." Padding across the ancient hardwood, he stepped up behind her and kissed her ear. "Take a breath, babe. We haven't had a proper good morning." Hand flattened against her stomach, he tossed the bra on the bed so he could caress her breast.

"Oh, Noah," she said, pushing back against him. "I don't have time for this."

Dropping his hand to play between her legs, he trailed his teeth along her shoulder. "You're already late. What's a few more minutes?"

Her back arched, her ass riding his erection. "A few more minutes might be okay." Noah rolled her clit, drawing the moan he craved. "I can definitely make time," she breathed, dropping her clothes to lock her hands on his hips.

"We need a condom, babe," he whispered in her ear, his breathing harsh as he held himself back.

"Where did we leave them?" she asked, cradling the base of his cock.

This was not the time for a scavenger hunt. Noah peered over her shoulder to see the box teetering on the edge of a bottom corner of the bed. Within reach, thank the sex gods. Ripping through the packaging, he sheathed himself in seconds and lifted Carrie to kneel on the bed, slamming inside her as soon as he had her in position. With a cry of ecstasy, she met the thrust, dropping her head to the covers.

His body tensed as her heat and scent surrounded him. She spread her knees farther apart and took him deep enough to make him see stars. Noah growled as power coiled through his body. Determined to hold on until she came first, he gritted his teeth, leaning forward to slide a finger between her legs. Carrie clenched down as the orgasm shot through her, and Noah let himself go, pulling her up off the bed to hold her to his chest.

This is mine, he thought, sinking his teeth into her shoulder while she shuddered against him. He would defeat his demons for this woman. Or die trying.

Though Carrie felt bad about skipping church and leaving Molly with Rosie for so long, she regretted nothing about how she'd spent the night. Or the morning. Once she'd managed to get her clothes on, something Noah seemed determined not to let happen, she'd found her phone at the base of the stairs where it must have fallen out of her pocket when Noah carried her in.

That was a nice memory. Petite or not, Carrie didn't get toted around by big, strapping men very often. In fact, *often* was the wrong word since she'd *never* been swept off her feet like that. Did it count as being swept if she actually jumped? Eh. The details didn't matter.

What *did* matter was that the night had been everything she'd hoped and more. When Noah looked at her, she felt wanted and sexy. When he touched her, her brain turned to mush and her body ignited. And then there was the beard. She totally understood the fascination with those now. Holy moly.

The little bit of battery left on the phone had been enough to read Lorelei's text.

Granny is taking Molly to church. No rush.

She'd even added the obvious emoticon in case Carrie missed the underlying message of *feel free to keep having sex*. In truth, she'd been tempted to do just that, but if they didn't spend some time apart, Carrie might lose the ability to walk. When she'd expressed that thought to Noah, he'd appeared quite proud of himself, but she'd caught the tell-tale stutter in his step as well. He hadn't been impervious to the night's rigorous activities, either.

The moment she stepped into Mamacita's Mexican Restaurant, Carrie spotted her daughter in a high chair straight ahead. Nodding to the hostess, she said, "I see my party right down there, thanks."

Navigating through the tables, she waved to Lorelei, who informed Molly that there was someone special behind her. The child's face lit up when she spotted her mother. "Hey there, baby." Carrie kissed the top of her head. "Did you have fun with Granny Rosie?"

Carrie's mother lived in Kentucky, her sister in New Mexico, and her brother occupied parts unknown on a sub somewhere in the Pacific. Her father still lived on the outskirts of town, but she'd broken ties with him years ago. Gary Lockwood had ruled his family with an iron fist and a steel-toed boot. No one had been spared, but her mother had endured the worst. Another reason Carrie had stayed with Patch. In her experience, women stayed no matter what. It wasn't until six months before his death that her mom had broken free of her abusive marriage and skipped town for a man she'd met online.

Carrie hadn't even known her mother knew how to use the Internet, let alone dating sites.

With her family all scattered to the winds, having surrogate family around helped fill a hole in Molly's life. And made Carrie feel less alone in the world. Some higher power had been smiling down on her the night Lorelei had saved her from another beating.

"So?" Lorelei said as Carrie took the seat across from her and opened her menu.

"I haven't had the fajitas for a while," she replied, keeping her eyes on the delicious options.

"No you don't, missy. Spill."

Carrie closed the menu. "I'm not sharing details with my daughter sitting right here."

Lorelei rolled her eyes. "She doesn't even speak English yet."

As if to prove her auntie wrong, Molly said, "Mum Mum Mum Mum."

"You're not helping, kid."

"It went well," Carrie shared. "Very, very well."

"As in 'I was home by midnight but smiling' well or 'I saw God several times' well?"

Unable to keep the pink from her cheeks, she said, "The second one."

"Whoot!" Lorelei exclaimed, raising the roof. "Do we need to buy you another box of con—"

"People can hear you," Carrie pointed out, flashing an awkward smile to the two older ladies at the next table over.

Lorelei waved to their neighbors. "They've had sex before. They can handle a little morning-after chatter."

"Maybe they can, but I'm not used to this."

"Not used to what?" she asked, tossing a corn chip into her mouth.

Carrie caught her menu before Molly could throw it into the air. "Until last summer, I never had friends like this. Girlfriends you could say anything to. The only reason I was so open in the limo yesterday was the champagne. Sharing intimate details is new for me."

"You don't have to tell me," Lorelei said, twirling the straw in her water glass. "I'm just happy to hear that you had a good time."

"Really?" Carrie didn't believe her for a second.

"Of course not," she said. "But I'm not going to force the details out of you. I might die of curiosity, but not for a few days at least."

That wasn't manipulative at all. "We can talk about it without going into detail, right? I mean, I can tell you that I didn't get your text until well after ten this morning because we were still . . . busy. He's so sweet and caring and when he holds me, I feel, I don't know, special, I guess. Protected."

"How serious is this?" Lorelei asked. "I thought we were talking casual fling with some awesome sex."

"I don't know. I've only known him for two weeks, really." Stating that fact aloud brought reality crashing in. "Holy crap. I just spent the night with a man I've only known for two weeks. What is wrong with me?"

Molly threw her toy key ring on the floor, clearly unhappy with the lack of attention.

"Chill your diaper, chickie," Lorelei said, bending to pick up the toy. "Your mommy is having a meltdown." To Carrie, she said, "You've known him for years, you just didn't see him for a long time. Even so, there's nothing wrong with sleeping with a man after two weeks. Some people barely wait two days. There's no written rule for that kind of thing."

"We *have* spent a lot of time together. Sort of." Two weeks or seven years, Carrie felt as if she'd known Noah forever. At the same time, there was so much of his life that she knew nothing about. He didn't like talking about his time in the service, and she didn't blame him, but what about family? Friends? Did he want to stay in Ardent Springs indefinitely? Did he want kids? And most of all, did he want more than just sex from her?

Lorelei covered Carrie's hand with her own. "You really like this guy, don't you?"

Unable to lie, she nodded her head. "I really like him."

Her friend sat back with concern in her eyes. "That changes things a bit."

Apprehension skittered down her back. "What does that mean?"

"I hate it when Spencer is right," the other woman said, ignoring Carrie's question.

"What is Spencer right about?"

Stirring her water once more, Lorelei said, "When I told him that we dropped you off with a box of condoms, he gave me the third degree. Wanted to know who the guy is and what I knew about him. I told him all I really knew was his name and that he'd been friends with Patch. As you can imagine, that didn't go over well."

Carrie tensed. "Noah is nothing like Patch."

"That may be true, but Spencer remembers him. Said he was a hothead with a rep for being an arrogant ass. I barely talked him out of driving over to get you."

Anger brewed to life. "Because, of course, I can't be trusted to know what is and isn't good for me, and I have to be watched and coddled and saved from my own bad decisions."

"Honey, that's not how it is."

"I get that I've earned the skepticism, but I won't let anyone insult Noah. He's a good man, Lorelei. He's been through hell and back, and he's still wonderful with Molly and makes me feel like I'm worth something again."

"You were always worth something." Lorelei waved the approaching waitress off. "We care about you, that's all. Spencer was being overprotective, but you can't blame him for wanting to protect you. He still blames himself for not seeing what Patch was doing to you."

What was it with the men in her life wanting to take the blame for something that had nothing to do with them?

"I appreciate what you and Spencer and everyone else have done for me and Molly. Lord knows where we'd be without you. But I don't need a keeper. And I won't stand for anyone being less than kind and respectful to Noah. Spencer doesn't have to like him, but he won't disrespect him either."

"Does Noah feel the same way about you?" she asked.

Doubt reared its ugly head. "I think so," she said. "I hope so."

With a nod, Lorelei said, "Then I hope so, too. You deserve to be happy. If Noah is the man to do that for you, then I'm all for him."

The support meant a lot. "Thank you. Now we should probably let our poor, hovering waitress come take our orders."

The plastic keys went flying again.

Lorelei retrieved them once more. "Throw them again, stinker, and they're staying on the floor."

Carrie smiled at her daughter's infectious giggle, but the barrage of doubts and fears now dancing through her brain stole her appetite. No way would she scare Noah off by demanding to know how he felt about her. Their farewell that morning had taken more than fifteen minutes because he'd refused to let her go. That had to mean something. Something more than physical pleasure.

She wasn't an idiot. If Noah wanted sex, he could drive into town and get it from anyone he wanted. He didn't need to bed the widow next door to get his rocks off. They'd made plans to see each other this evening, which bolstered Carrie's confidence and put a smile on her face.

Once her friends met him, all of this would go away. They'd see that Noah was good for her. They'd come around eventually.

∿

"Molly, honey, don't run over Wilson's tail." Carrie would expect the cat to have learned by now and keep to higher elevations when the walker was in use.

"That cat is huge," Noah pointed out, popping a cherry tomato between his teeth. "I've never seen a cat that big."

This was not a new sentiment. Every person who entered Carrie's house, be it the cable installer or her friends, commented on the size of her feline. And to all she gave the same response.

"He's just big-boned is all. Huh, Wilson? You're the perfect size, buddy. Don't let anyone give you a complex."

The black cat hefted himself onto the back of the couch.

"I don't think big bones are his problem."

"Shh . . ." Carrie dropped a handful of the tomatoes into a salad bowl. "Leave my poor cat alone. He's beautiful just the way he is."

"So are you," Noah said, taking her by surprise. He wasn't the type to toss around romantic compliments.

133

"Flattery won't get you out of peeling these potatoes," she said, pointing toward the bag at the end of the counter. "We had a deal."

Noah pulled three knives from the block before he found the paring knife. "I'm willing to work for my supper." Lifting the spuds, he said, "You got a couple bowls so I can do this at the table? There isn't much room in here for two of us."

When picking out her trailer, Carrie hadn't expected to have a man helping out in the kitchen. Even if by some miracle she did risk her heart again, in her world, men did not participate in food preparation.

Pulling a large mixing bowl from a bottom cupboard, she said, "You can pull the garbage can over for the skins and drop the clean spuds in here."

Without argument, Noah took his food and tools to the table. They'd been working in silence for nearly a minute when he said, "I ran into Patch's baby sister about a week ago."

Kyra Farmer had never been one of Carrie's favorite people, and the feeling was mutual. Ever since the spoiled brat had demanded that Carrie buy her alcohol, and then proceeded to throw an unholy fit when told no, the two had been at odds. Even years later, no family gathering passed without Kyra sliding a backhanded insult in her sister-in-law's direction. Carrie had fired back only once and had paid a painful price later that night.

"Really?" she asked, thankful he couldn't see her face. No matter what he knew now, Patch and Noah had been friends for a long time, and that meant that Noah knew the entire Farmer family.

"How often do you see his family?" he asked.

"Not often," she answered, bending to check the chicken in the oven.

"Why not?" he asked. "Patch was Althea's only son. No matter what he did to you, she should be part of Molly's life, don't you think?"

Spinning to face him, she said, "The last time I took my daughter to see her grandmother she was five months old. As babies do, she got curious and stuck her fingers in Althea's ashtray. Before I could react, that woman smacked my child's hand hard enough to leave a welt that lasted several hours." Reaching into an upper cupboard, she slammed two plates onto the counter. "Patch wasn't an anomaly in that family. They're all cut from the same cloth."

Shaking from the outburst, Carrie leaned on the counter behind her only to leap forward when the hot oven door touched her legs.

"Careful, honey," he said, dropping a half-peeled potato into the bowl and rising to his feet. "Are you all right?"

"I'm fine." Embarrassed, she opened the silverware drawer and withdrew two forks, two butter knives, and one of Molly's colorful spoons. "I don't want to talk about that family anymore."

"You don't have to," Noah said, coming up behind her to slide his hands down her arms. "Forget I said anything."

Anger fading, Carrie turned to face him, pressing her forehead to his chest. "I shouldn't have snapped like that."

"My fault for sticking my nose where it doesn't belong." With one finger beneath her chin, he nudged her head up. "You're a good mother, Carrie."

A compliment that meant a great deal more than the last one.

"Thank you," she whispered, rising on tiptoe as Noah leaned down for a kiss. The moment he deepened the connection, something solid slammed into their legs.

"What the—"

"Language," she said, looking down into the face of her smiling cherub. "Did I mention she's deadly with the walker?"

Instead of complaining about the interruption, Noah swooped Molly into the air, carrying her into the living room while making propeller sounds. "It's the amazing flying baby. Look at her go." Peals of laughter filled the trailer as he brought her down just enough to blow raspberries on her belly. Molly smacked both hands against his forehead, and he lifted her for another flight around the room.

Carrie watched the pair play, drinking in the sound of Noah's carefree laughter. She'd never heard him laugh like that before. Never seen him this relaxed and happy. When he dropped onto the couch to bounce the baby on his knee, something scary yet undeniable flowed through her chest. She wasn't just in deep. She was in love.

Chapter 14

Noah had found his magic pill. In the week since Carrie first occupied his bed, only two nightmares had disturbed his sleep. And neither featured the widow and her little girl. He still didn't sleep much, but that had more to do with starting his evenings in *her* bed and then spending the rest of the night wanting her from *his*.

Before they'd moved activities to her place, he and Carrie had discussed the issue of Molly. At ten months old (as of three days earlier), she didn't understand what they were doing and wasn't likely to have a problem with her newest spoiler taking up residence. But Carrie still felt uncomfortable letting Noah stay the night. She and the child had a pattern that included bringing Molly into her bed if she woke in the wee hours of the morning. Eventually, that might work with three in the bed, but he respected the single mother's wishes and took his leave each night, typically somewhere around midnight.

He appreciated that Carrie never insisted on traditional dates. Crowds weren't his thing, and he'd much rather spend a couple of hours with her curled against him on the couch than sit across from her in some restaurant. She made no demands. Never talked about the future or asked questions that he couldn't answer. She had to be curious. At times, he'd even been tempted to share some of his experiences. To help her understand the shit in his head. But to do so would be shifting his burden onto her shoulders, and he refused to do that to her.

She had enough baggage of her own.

Today was her ex-husband's wedding. When she'd told him about the time and place, Noah had feared she'd expect him to go with her. To his relief, she'd never extended the invitation, saving him the need to turn her down. A church full of strangers sizing up the hairy oaf with the pretty widow was not his idea of a fun Saturday afternoon.

Around the time he assumed she'd be leaving, a white Ford Edge pulled down her drive. A short redhead climbed from the passenger side and crossed around the front to join the driver. The woman wore jeans and a black T-shirt. Not exactly wedding attire. The driver looked like a politician with perfect blond hair and a tan sport jacket. The redhead straightened the guy's tie before heading for Carrie's front door.

Curiosity getting the best of him, Noah stepped onto the porch as Mr. Fancy Pants strolled up the drive. If the constant tightening of the tie and tucking of the shirt were any indication, the man was nervous. But what the hell was he nervous about?

Carrie answered the knock at her door and stepped into the sun wearing a pretty blue number. She'd swept her hair into a clip on the back of her head and fought the wind to keep the few stray strands out of her eyes. When the driver climbed the stairs, he gave Carrie a hug that made Noah want to rip his head off. He descended his own steps, cracking his knuckles on the way down.

Over Suit Boy's shoulder, Carrie spotted him and broke the hug, but the stranger kept his arm around her, seemingly clueless to the danger lurking across the fence. The shorter woman carried on a short discussion with Carrie before disappearing into the house. The two remaining outside headed for the Ford, appearing for all intents and purposes like a couple embarking on a date.

"Hey," Noah said. "What's going on?"

"I'm going to the wedding, remember?"

"Yeah. I remember. And him?" he asked, gesturing with his chin toward the dude beside her.

"I'm Dale Lambdon," Pretty Boy offered, extending a hand. "I'm the lucky guy taking Carrie to the wedding."

Noah crossed his arms to keep from ripping the asshole to shreds. "Is that so?"

Dale awkwardly lowered his hand. "I'm glad to know there's someone out here with Carrie now. I worried about her living so far from town all alone."

"You can stop worrying," he said. "She's well protected."

"Good. Good."

"Dale, could you give me one minute with Noah, please?"

The interloper smiled. "Sure. I'll wait in the car."

"Thanks." Carrie stepped closer to the gate. "Are you angry?"

"You have a date for the wedding?"

"I'm going with Dale, yes. But—"

"That's all I need to know." Noah spun, gritting his teeth to keep his temper in check. He wanted to punch something. Preferably Pretty Boy's face.

"Noah, wait. Let me explain."

Slamming into the house, he marched straight through to the back door, never breaking stride. He'd hung a punching bag in the barn earlier in the week. No time like the present to break it in. Before he reached his destination, Noah heard tires crunch over gravel as the Edge backed out of Carrie's driveway. A steady drumbeat kicked in his temple as he dragged the sliding door open, and without reaching for the overhead light, he plugged his phone into the speaker and cranked the music.

As his fists connected with the bag, Noah cursed himself for being a fool. No wonder she didn't need him to take her on fancy dates. She had that duty covered.

The only reason Carrie climbed into Dale's car was because she knew Noah needed time to cool off. When she returned in a few hours, he'd have calmed down and would be more willing to listen. Less than a mile down the road, his stricken expression stuck with her. He'd been angry. There'd been no doubt about that. But he'd also been hurt. Telling him ahead of time that Dale was taking her to the wedding would have been the smart thing to do. Except she'd assumed that he'd know this date meant nothing. They'd spent every night together. Made love in her bed countless times.

He had to know that she wouldn't spend her nights with him and still see someone else. Then again, she'd done this before, right? She'd cheated on her husband. Once a cheater, always a cheater. Wasn't that how the saying went?

"Go back," she said.

"What?" Dale let his foot off the gas. "Did you forget to tell Mya something? We can call her."

"No." Carrie shook her head, twisting in her seat to see Noah's house. "Take me back. I can't do this."

Dale pulled off the road and put the SUV in park. "You can't do what? Carrie, what's going on?"

Desperate to make him turn around, Carrie looked her driver in the eye. "I'm sorry, Dale, but I never should have let this go on so long.

You're a great guy, and you'll find a great girl someday. But that girl isn't me. Now, please. Take me back to Noah."

"But what about the wedding?"

"I don't care about the wedding right now. Turn around or let me out so I can run on my own."

"I will never understand women," he mumbled, making a U-turn. Before the vehicle came to a full stop, Carrie's feet were on the ground. "I'm sorry, Dale. I'm really sorry," she called, pulling off her heels so she could run across the grass. Relieved to find the front door unlocked, she pushed her way inside. "Noah! Noah, where are you?"

Silence answered.

"The barn." A shoe in each hand, Carrie charged out the back door and across the yard. Music blared through the old wooden walls. Smart enough not to make the same mistake twice, she went for the speaker first. The music cut off, and she searched the dim interior to find him. "Noah, please let me explain."

"I'm not interested," came a voice from the back corner, heavy with emotion.

God, she'd really hurt him.

Stepping around a partially assembled motorcycle, she said, "Noah, I agreed to go to the wedding with Dale weeks before you moved in."

"Good for Dale."

"He's been taking me out for months, and I thought if I kept spending time with him that I'd eventually feel what he feels. He's a nice guy. He's safe. I thought that's what I wanted." Her eyes adjusted to the low light, and she spotted him with his forehead pressed to a giant bag. "But I was wrong. About all of it."

"No, you were right," he said, stepping back and throwing two quick punches at the bag. "You deserve someone safe."

"Noah, you have to listen to me." Three more punches. "Dammit, Noah Winchester. The reason I know I'll never love Dale Lambdon, or anyone else, is because I'm in love with you."

The brutal attack on the bag ceased, and his eyes locked on hers. "What did you say?"

Taking the risk, she repeated the words. "I'm in love with you, Noah. I don't want anyone else. And you don't have to say it back or worry that things will cha—"

Before Carrie could finish her sentence, Noah closed the distance between them to lift her off her feet. The kiss said everything she needed to hear, and when they finally came up for air, Carrie's arms were wrapped around his neck, a delicate silver heel next to each of his ears while her feet dangled nearly a foot off the ground.

"There's a good chance you'll regret this someday," he said.

She hushed him with a quick kiss. "You'll never hurt me, Noah. Not if you can help it. We'll deal with the rest together."

He stole her breath with another kiss before setting her back on her feet. "What about the wedding?" he asked.

"We'd better get you cleaned up or we're going to miss the whole thing."

As she expected, he argued. "I'm not cut out for stuff like that."

"You're my man," she said. "Let me show you off." Seeing the doubt lingering in his eyes, she added, "We'll sneak in the back, eat a few peanuts at the reception, and come back home. I promise to make it as painless as possible."

Sweeping an arm beneath her legs, he cradled her against his chest and marched out of the barn. "I don't have a fancy suit like your politician guy."

Carrie laughed. "Dale works for the sheriff's department. And you don't need a suit. Jeans and a nice shirt will be fine."

Setting her down on the back porch, Noah shot her a heart-stopping smile. "I can do that."

"I still say it's weird to be invited to your ex's wedding," Noah mumbled before reaching for his fourth cookie. "But these are the best damn cookies I've ever had."

"You'll get used to the weirdness," Carrie replied. "The rest of us have. Mostly. And Lorelei makes those cookies. Amazing, aren't they?"

"The one in white bakes?"

Carrie chuckled. "I know she doesn't look like the domestic type, but she's a whiz with a whisk. You want to go check out the cupcakes?"

Noah surveyed the dessert table on the other side of the room. "Too many people." He'd been lucky that the cookie table occupied a remote corner where he could stand with his back to the wall. "I'm good here if you want to go talk to your friends."

"I'm not leaving you," she said. "We'll wait until they come to us."

Not wanting to keep her from the party, he said, "I'm a big boy. You don't need to babysit me."

She hooked her arm through his and looked up. "I like being with you, thank you very much."

Leaning down to whisper in her ear, Noah said, "And I like being with you."

"What are *you* doing here?"

Noah looked up to find the shelter board lady staring at him as if he'd rolled in a pile of shit before walking in.

"Carrie, tell me this isn't what it looks like."

"Good afternoon, Meredith," his girl said, her smile never faltering. "If it looks like Noah is with me, then it's definitely what it looks like. How are you today?"

The older woman's lip actually curled in distaste. "Why are you wasting your time with this cretin?"

Carrie dropped the niceties. "If you can't be civil, then feel free to mingle elsewhere, Meredith. Noah is my date, and I will not tolerate you insulting him."

Pride filled his chest as the snooty witch moved along.

"And I thought seeing you naked was a turn-on."

Carrie exhaled as she turned her back to the crowd. "I can't believe I just did that. She's going to rip me to pieces at the next board meeting."

"You can hold your own," he said, rubbing her back. "You're stronger than you give yourself credit for."

"I didn't used to be."

"So you *are* here," a slender blonde said, whisking Carrie into a quick hug. "We saved seats at the wedding but never saw you come in. When Dale walked in alone, I was afraid something had happened to Molly." As if belatedly noticing him, she turned wide eyes on Noah. "Oh, this is making more sense now."

Skipping over the Dale part, Carrie made the introductions. "Noah, this is Haleigh Mitchner and Cooper Ridgeway. Haleigh is the doctor who delivered Molly, and Cooper is the one I said you should talk to about your restoration business."

"You restore cars?" the friendly giant asked. It wasn't often Noah met a man who beat him in height.

"Motorcycles," he corrected. "Or that's the plan, anyway. I restored my '96 Harley after some kid trashed it. I've gotten lucky and found a frame with the tank intact for a '75 Ironhead, so that's next."

"I've got a buddy in Gallatin who found a '79. She's a beauty, but he paid a fortune for her."

"While you boys talk shop," Haleigh said, "I'm going to steal Carrie for just a minute."

Before either man could argue, the women wandered off. Noah must have been obvious about trying to keep an eye on Carrie.

"She'll be back. Hal is just pumping her for information."

"About what?"

"You." Cooper grinned. "Carrie seems to really like you."

"Is that what you've heard?"

Instead of answering, the big guy said, "You know those divider things in limos? The window between the driver and the passengers?"

"I haven't spent much time in limousines, but sure."

Cooper shook his head. "Not soundproof."

The weekend before flashed to mind. "That must have made for a long night for you."

"My sister was in that car. My drunk, desperate-for-sex sister."

Noah smacked him on the back. "I'm sorry, man."

Laughing at his own suffering, Cooper said, "You interested in a beer?"

Feeling as if he'd made a new ally, Noah decided to peel himself off the wall. "Nope. But I could go for a soda. Lead the way."

Chapter 15

"First of all," Haleigh said, "what the heck did you say to Mom? She pulled me aside in a huff and claimed you're jeopardizing your place on the board."

Carrie simmered at the insinuation. "She can't kick me off the board because she doesn't like my boyfriend. This shelter was my idea, not hers."

"Whoa. Did you say boyfriend? That explains Dale's long face."

"That makes two things I haven't handled well today." Carrie pulled Haleigh away from the crowd. "I knew that Noah would hate an event like this, and I didn't want to hurt Dale's feelings, so I kept my mouth shut hoping it would all work out. And then Noah saw me leaving with Dale, and he got mad—I thought for a minute it was going to get ugly—but I could see that he was also hurt and, well, I made Dale turn around and take me back."

"The poor guy didn't see it coming, did he?"

"Completely clueless. But I never did more than kiss him, and that was a peck on the lips." Carrie spotted Noah and Cooper headed to the bar. "What man doesn't get a clue from that?"

"Dale, I guess. What are you looking at?"

Carrie stepped out of the corner. "Noah just went with Cooper to the bar."

Haleigh followed her gaze. "You say that like it's a big deal."

"Noah doesn't like crowds. That's why we were standing out of the way." She craned her neck to see what was in his glass and realized the men were headed their way. "Here they come."

"Quick. Tell me what you said to Mom," Haleigh whispered.

"She called Noah a cretin, and I basically told her to buzz off. They had a run-in on the job site, but you know your mother. She walked in with guns blazing, demanding answers and a tour. Noah didn't know who she was and basically told her the same thing I just did, only I'm guessing there was more profanity involved."

"I'd have paid to see that."

"And I'd have paid to avoid it."

"What are you two whispering about back here?" asked Cooper, handing a soft drink to Haleigh.

"The usual," she replied. "Discussing whose purse doesn't match her shoes and taking bets on how long the newlyweds will stick around before making a break for it."

Cooper searched the crowd, presumably for the happy couple. "If I know Spencer, he has the truck running and waiting at the back door."

"She spent months planning this," Carrie pointed out. "He has to let her enjoy it."

With a raised brow, Noah said, "If I were the groom, I'd be more interested in enjoying something else."

Carrie blushed, pretending she didn't notice the knowing exchange between her friends.

"Have you met the bride and groom yet?" Cooper asked.

"We don't have to do that today," Carrie said.

Dark brows drew together as Noah sent her a questioning look.

"Sure you do." Waving a hand over his head, Cooper flagged down the host and hostess.

As they approached, Carrie tugged on Noah's arm until he bent to her level. "Be nice. I don't know what Spencer is going to say."

With no time to respond, Noah straightened and accepted the offered handshake as Cooper introduced him. "Congratulations on your big day," he offered.

"Thanks," the groom replied. "I didn't know you were coming."

Carrie shot Lorelei a *make him behave* look.

"What Spencer means to say is that we're glad you could make it, Noah. Carrie has told us a lot about you."

Addressing his ex, Spencer said, "I thought you were coming with Dale."

"Change of plans," she replied with a nervous laugh. "Lorelei, Noah loves your cookies." Yeah. That didn't sound weird *at all*. "You guys must be leaving soon. Gotta get a head start on that drive to Gatlinburg."

Staring holes through Noah, Spencer said, "We have time."

"My dad has nothing but good things to say about you," the bride tried again, digging an elbow into her new husband's side.

"Your dad?" Noah asked. They'd crept into the wedding somewhere in the middle, which meant Noah never saw who escorted Lorelei down the aisle.

"Mike is Lorelei's father," Carrie explained. "We should probably find him and say hello."

Before she could push Noah out of the line of fire, Spencer cut them off. "Carrie has a lot of friends around here. Friends who wouldn't think twice about stepping in if someone hurts her."

Every muscle in Carrie's body froze as tension crackled in the air. This was it. Either Noah would walk away because she wasn't worth this hassle, or her ex-husband was going to die on his wedding day.

But instead of throwing a punch, Noah slid his hand into Carrie's and pulled her close. "I'm grateful for what you've done for her, but so long as I've got breath in my body, no one will ever hurt her again."

"See?" Lorelei said, flashing Noah a satisfied grin. "I told you. Now can we end this pissing match and get back to celebrating our marriage?"

Spencer sized up his opponent for several more seconds before wrapping an arm around his wife. "It's time for a toast from the best man anyway," he said, once again offering a hand to Noah. "Welcome back, Winchester."

Carrie let out the breath she'd been holding as Noah accepted the truce, saying, "Thanks. It's good to be home."

One hysterical speech from the best man, followed by a more poignant one from the maid of honor, seemed to signal the end of the party. Noah and Carrie let the mass of bodies file out first, and then they skirted the crowd to find a spot near the front and watched Spencer kiss his bride like a man unconcerned with offending the more prudish in attendance. Noah ducked his head when handfuls of birdseed flew through the air.

As the shaving cream–covered Dodge pickup disappeared in the distance, Carrie looked down the front of her dress. "My bra could double as a bird feeder."

Leaning forward to assess the situation, Noah said, "I can help you clean that out."

Cutting off the show, she failed to hide the interest in her eyes. "Always willing to help a girl out, aren't you?"

"Not any girl," he murmured, holding her close. "Just my girl."

Ice-blue eyes went soft as she tracked two fingers up his chest. "Thank you for what you did earlier."

"What did I do?" Noah asked, too distracted by her touch to think straight.

"Made peace with Spencer. He was a jerk and you could have been a jerk back, but you weren't."

If the encounter had happened somewhere else, or even before Carrie had said she loved him, Noah might have handled the situation differently. But today appeared to be Spencer Boyd's lucky day in more ways than one.

Leading Carrie to the parking lot, he said, "I can't blame the guy for looking out for you."

"I can," she said, tucking her arm through his. "You and Cooper seemed to hit it off."

"The guy's been through a lot," Noah said, growing serious. "I felt bad for him."

Stopping, she said, "What are you talking about? Cooper's the happiest guy I know, other than Spencer."

Pressing his lips beside her ear, he whispered, "That little window inside your limo wasn't soundproof."

Carrie gasped. "No."

"Oh yes." He tugged to get her moving again. "The poor guy might be scarred for life."

"His sister . . ."

"From what I can tell, that was the worst part." They reached his truck, and an idea struck as Noah opened the passenger door. "Is that babysitter expecting you home right away?"

"I didn't give her a time when I'd be home, but she'll know the wedding wouldn't last into the night."

Noah didn't need that long to accomplish his plan. "Can you give her a call and see if she'll give us another hour?"

Suspicious, she said, "What do you have in mind?"

"I want to show you something." He lifted her into the passenger seat. "I'll have you home by sundown. Promise."

"Now you have me curious." Reaching into her purse, she said, "Let me call and see what she says."

By the time Noah climbed behind the wheel, Carrie had gotten the sitter on the phone.

"We're going to make another stop. Do you mind staying a little longer?" He waited out the response until Carrie said, "I know I didn't handle that well." Another pause. "Mya, he doesn't have to be alone. If you'd— Okay, I'll butt out. But give us an hour, and then you can buy him a six-pack and tell him all the reasons I was wrong for him anyway." A second later Carrie gave him a thumbs-up. "Thanks, Mya. I really appreciate this."

As she tucked the phone back into her purse, Noah said, "Did I hear that right? Your babysitter has a thing for the goody-two-shoes guy?"

"It's complicated," she said, locking her seat belt. "Now where are we going?"

"You'll see." After checking behind his seat for the old blanket he kept for emergencies, Noah snapped his own belt into place.

"Is it far?" Carrie asked.

"Not far at all," he answered.

For several miles, Carrie had been certain that Noah was playing a joke on her since they were headed straight for the farm. But then he made a left onto a dirt road she'd never noticed before. A rusty metal gate blocked the entrance, forcing Noah to stop the truck.

"I'll be right back," he said.

"Noah, this looks like private property."

"It is," he said. "It's mine."

Closing his door before she could ask more questions, he unchained the gate and swung it open. When he returned, she said, "I don't understand."

"Two minutes, hon. Hold on for two more minutes."

Holding on became a literal requirement as the truck swayed from side to side, navigating the narrow, crater-lined path that led into a thick copse of trees. An hour ago, she'd trusted Noah unconditionally. Now she wasn't so sure. If there was ever a spot to hide a body, this was it.

"Have you brought anyone back here before?" she asked, horror-movie plots circling through her mind.

"No one but Zeke. We came back here a lot when we were kids."

Since Zeke had lived to see adulthood, Carrie felt a little better. Until they hit a pothole the size of the Grand Canyon and Carrie stopped worrying about being killed to focus all her energy on not tossing Lorelei's delicious cookies onto Noah's dashboard. Breathing deeply, in through her nose and out through her mouth, she gasped when the gnarled trees opened to reveal a beautiful field of swaying reeds dotted by the tallest pussy willows she'd ever seen.

The land appeared untouched while the lane finally leveled out and Noah pulled through to the edge of a motionless pond. He spun the truck around to back up as close to the water as he could get, then tugged a blanket from behind the seat. "This is it. The prettiest spot in Tennessee and the best fishing this side of the Mississippi. At least it used to be."

Carrie undid her seat belt and twisted to look out the back window. In the distance she spotted a giant willow tree that looked familiar, as if she'd seen it before. A silly thought. All trees looked alike, and she'd definitely never been anywhere near this one.

"Stay in the truck until I come around," he ordered. "The snakes are probably pretty thick right now."

Noah's secret place dropped several levels on the pretty meter. Carrie did not do snakes. In the year she'd lived in the trailer, she'd encountered two, and both times had called Spencer in a panic to come get rid of them. He'd teased her mercilessly about her phobia, but Carrie didn't care so long as the nasty creatures disappeared.

By the time Noah opened her door, she'd tucked her feet under her butt as if something might slither over her toes inside the truck.

"Ready?" he said.

Carrie shook her head. "I don't like snakes."

"Honey, that was just a warning." He kicked at the high grass around his legs. "There's nothing out here right now. Come here and I'll lift you into the back."

Unwilling to chance it, she searched for an escape. "I'll go through the window," she said, sliding the back glass to one side.

"Are you craz—" Noah started, but Carrie was already through to her hips. At which point, she got stuck.

"Open the window more," she yelled.

Noah had the nerve to laugh. "That's all the farther it goes, babe. I tried to tell you."

Too angry to be mortified, she said, "Then climb up here and pull me through."

"Just scoot back into the cab and I'll get you."

Balancing with her hands in the truck bed, Carrie yelled over her shoulder. "I'm not getting down there with the snakes."

"All right then," he said, amusement in every word. "You asked for it."

Instead of climbing into the truck bed to pull her through, Noah shoved her from behind, remembering at the last moment to grab her ankles before she could land on her head. With what little dignity she had left, Carrie crawled forward on her hands until her toes touched down in the truck bed.

Peering through the window, he said, "That would have been a lot easier my way."

Carrie clapped the dirt off her hands, refusing to meet his eye. "I told you. I don't like snakes."

Noah exited the truck, closing the door and then jumping over the side with the blanket. "Scoot over so I can spread this out."

As if the blanket mattered now that her dress had dusted the bottom of the bed. She took a seat on the tire well, examining the ground behind her. "Can they climb up here?"

"Snakes can go anywhere they want," he said, straightening out the last corner.

Wrong answer.

Carrie jumped to her feet, hopping into the middle of the blanket. "I want to go home."

Pulling her against him, Noah said, "You are home."

"What?"

He pointed over the ridge, to the left of the big willow. "The farmhouse is seventy acres that way."

"Oh." Surveying the area, she said, "That's the tree I can see out my back window."

"That's the one. My great-great-grandfather planted it in 1928. That part of the farm would turn into a marsh every time it rained, so he planted the willow to soak up the water."

She hadn't realized the farm had been in his family for so long. "How many acres do you have?"

"About one sixty, give or take." He shrugged, staring out over the field. "The back forty got sold off years ago. It's perfect pasture land, so it's good for cows and horses. Seemed a shame for it to go to waste."

While Noah watched the willow sway in the wind, Carrie watched him. She could see the pride in his eyes. Feel his body relax against her.

"You love this place," she said.

His lashes lowered as he looked down. "I thought that coming back here, to the farm, would quiet the voices. I should have known it wouldn't be that easy."

"They might fade in time."

"They might," he agreed, but looked doubtful. "This is where Granddaddy taught Zeke and me how to fish. We spent entire summers on these banks, getting burned to a crisp, eaten up with chiggers, and dodging copperheads." Carrie shivered at the reminder that they weren't alone. "I should have left off that last one." Shifting her backward, he said, "Time to have a seat."

Carrie remained obstinate. "I don't know."

Noah settled below the window and pulled her onto his lap. "I can protect you better from down here." When he wrapped his arms around her, letting her head rest on his shoulder, Carrie gave up the fight. "There now. Isn't that better?"

She nodded, taking in the view. "You're right," she said. "This is beautiful."

"The second-prettiest thing I've seen today."

A breeze kicked up, but she stayed warm, surrounded by his body heat. "Thanks for going to the wedding with me."

"Thanks for ditching your date and taking me instead."

Cringing, she said, "I still feel bad about that."

Noah squeezed her tighter. "I don't. Fancy Pants can get his own girl. This one's mine."

Too emotional to respond, Carrie nestled into his arms and enjoyed the brilliant work of art forming on the horizon.

Chapter 16

Noah had taken up the habit of making grocery runs on Sunday mornings after realizing that church services meant empty aisles and no lines. The day after the wedding, as he carried a case of soda, lunch meat, bread, and a gallon of milk to his car, a flier caught his eye on the bulletin board near the exit, and an idea brewed to life. He ripped a slip from the bottom that included a contact phone number with the plan of calling from his truck. Before he could make that happen, his cell rang in his back pocket, requiring him to hurl the Coke and plastic bags into the truck bed to free up his hands.

The ID showed his mother's number. He hadn't called her in weeks.

"Well, hell," he said before answering. "Hey, Ma."

"So you do remember you have a mother." Sarcasm was his mother's first language.

"Yeah. Been busy."

"I would say, 'Too busy for your mother?' but then I'd sound like an old nag. And speaking of old, you do remember what's coming up this week, don't you?"

Noah leaned his back against the truck. "It's your birthday, Ma."

"And you haven't been home for my birthday in more years than I can count," she said, as if Noah didn't remember spending five years in hell. "Because I clearly need a reason to get you over here, I'm throwing a little get-together on Saturday. And before you tactlessly point it out, yes, I'm throwing my own birthday party. The only gift I want is you sitting beside me while I blow out my candles. Is that too much to ask?"

"No, Ma. I'll be there."

"Good. Now I hear you attended the Pratchett/Boyd wedding last weekend." How had he forgotten the gossip lines in this town? "Rumor has it you were with Patch's wife. Is that true?"

Pinching the bridge of his nose, Noah suppressed an expletive. "It's true."

"Was that doing a kindness for an old friend's widow or something else?"

Lying would be pointless. "Something else," he said.

A weighted pause hung on the line. "Then you need to bring her to the party."

"Ma, there's—"

"Three o'clock. Don't be late. Love you, buddy."

The line went dead, and Noah stared at the phone in his hand. How had he not seen that one coming? At the risk of pissing off dear old mother, he'd ask Carrie if she wanted to attend the party, but if she said no, which any intelligent person would, he'd show up alone and deal with the consequences. A force of nature with a generous heart and a no-bullshit attitude, Lydia Winchester could intimidate a four-star general without breaking a sweat. Carrie wouldn't stand a chance if Ma decided she wasn't the girl for his boy.

Not that Noah needed or cared about his mother's approval. She'd rarely liked his previous choices, but that had never stopped him from doing whatever the hell he pleased.

Climbing behind the wheel, he dragged the wadded-up slip of paper from his pocket and dialed the number. When a woman answered, he explained where he'd seen the flier and asked if the item was still for sale. A minute later, he had an address and a plan to put into motion.

~

"Hey, Carrie," said Dale, catching her in the fellowship hall contemplating the doughnut selections. "Can I talk to you for a minute?"

"Of course," she said, nervous about his intentions but aware that she owed him at least a real conversation. "Do you want to sit down?"

"Sure." He seemed surprised by the offer, but led the way to a back table and pulled a chair out for her. "Here you go."

"Thanks." Carrie tucked her dress under her legs as she sat. When Dale took the seat next to her, she said, "I want to apologize for how I handled things yesterday. I'm surprised you're willing to talk to me at all after the way I treated you."

With a self-effacing shrug, he said, "You aren't the first woman to dump me, Carrie. The first to bolt from my car at a sprint, but not the first to dump me."

"I must have looked like a crazy person."

"Just crazy in love." A genuine smile softened his face. "Noah Winchester is a lucky guy. And not that I don't see the obvious differences between us, but I thought you might tell me what went wrong."

"Excuse me?"

"In the end, I'd like to think that we're still friends, right?"

If he didn't hate her, she saw no reason that couldn't be true. "I hope so."

"Then as a friend, tell me where I messed up. Was there something I did or didn't do? At the risk of sounding pathetic, you're the fifth woman to break up with me in less than three years. I could continue on my clueless way, but I've decided to look at things from a more scientific angle. Gathering data, I guess you can say."

Carrie looked around for a hidden camera. "Are you serious?"

Dale leaned forward in his chair. "Mya is the only other female friend I trust, and she says there's nothing wrong with me. That it's the women I choose."

Trying not to be offended, she said, "I'm not sure it's all one side or the other. Sometimes two people just aren't right for each other."

"Five, Carrie. And the common denominator is me."

Choosing her words carefully, she toyed with the hem of her dress. "I don't have any idea why the other four women didn't work out, but I've thought a bit about why I couldn't seem to find a spark between us, and it really has nothing to do with you as a person, Dale. You're kind and sweet, and you're going to make the right girl very happy someday."

"But?" he said.

She glanced around to ensure no one would overhear. "The years I was with Patch, when neighbors would call the police, you were often the first one to show up."

"I was doing my job."

"And you were great. But you watched me make excuses while dabbing at a bloody lip. You witnessed the most humiliating moments of my life, and though you've never treated me with anything less than respect, the truth is, you know too much. I can't be a different me with you. I can't be a new version because you know the real story. You know the weak woman who stayed with a monster."

Dale balanced his elbows on his knees. "You talk about it as if *you* were the monster. You weren't weak, and you weren't to blame for anything that happened to you. I see it all the time. The excuses, the hidden shame, when the jerk throwing the punches is the one with something to be ashamed of."

Needing him to understand, she said, "Right or not, I carry that shame to this day. It's the ugliest thing about me, and you know it better than anyone else. That's what went wrong. Our history got in the way. And I'm sorry for that, because you really are a good man, Dale."

Leaning back with a sigh, he shook his head. "I should be relieved to know it wasn't anything I did, but this doesn't help me figure out the other four dumpings."

"You could call them up and ask them," she offered with a smile.

"I don't like any of them as much as I like you." He placed a quick kiss on her cheek. "I hope this Noah guy knows what he has. And if he ever gets out of line, call me. He's bigger, but I can bring backup."

Carrie laughed as a weight lifted off her heart. "Can I give you a little advice?" she asked.

"I'm all ears."

"Sometimes when you look too hard for something, you don't realize that it's right under your nose."

Dale narrowed his eyes. "That sounds like a riddle."

"Just think about it," she said.

Noah hadn't thought his plan through very well. When he arrived at the given address, the lady had taken his money and directed him to the backyard before closing the door in his face. Which meant he'd had to disassemble the thing himself and carry the pieces around to the truck, while attempting to memorize how to put them back together. Not sure he'd be able to finish the task before Carrie and Molly returned from church, he'd sent her a text suggesting she take her time, and, whatever she did, not to look into her backyard before Noah gave the okay.

By sheer will, or possibly a Sunday miracle, he'd screwed the last piece into place minutes before Carrie's car pulled into the drive.

"Molly fell asleep in the baby room, so I let her finish the nap before coming home," she said. "What in the world are you doing in my backyard?" Midway through unbuckling the child's car seat, she popped out of the car and lowered her voice. "Please tell me you didn't get her a pony."

"No," he said. "We'll wait another year for that."

Carrie rolled her eyes. "You're crazy."

As soon as she lifted Molly from the seat, the baby reached for Noah, and as had become routine, he lifted her right up to his shoulders. "I've got an early birthday present for you, princess."

"Her birthday is two months away," Carrie reminded him, dropping the diaper bag on the bottom porch step before following him around the trailer. "We hardly ever go back here."

"Watch for snakes," Noah said, picking up his pace.

"Not funny!" she yelled. And then she stopped beside him, seeing what he'd done. "Oh my gosh. Noah. You got her a swing set."

"It's a starter," he explained. "We'll upgrade to one of those fancy wooden ones eventually, but for now this little plastic one will get her started."

Molly kicked her feet. "Dow dow dow."

"I'll put you down." Noah set her at the top of the blue slide and kept his hands close as she made her way to the ground, catching her before she got grass stains on her church clothes. "Let's put you in a swing where you can't get so dirty." Used to being slotted into the walker, Molly straightened her legs and dropped into the special seat with no issues. "There you go," he said, pushing her into motion.

To his surprise, Carrie remained at the corner of the house.

"What's wrong?" he called.

She shook her head, staring at the giant toy.

Well, hellfire. Now he'd really screwed up. "I can take it back down," he said, attempting to pry Molly out of the swing.

"No," Carrie said, stepping close enough for him to see the tears. "It's perfect."

"If it's perfect, why are you crying?" he asked.

"I just . . ." she started. "This is . . ." Running her hand along the edge of the slide, she said, "It's silly, but I resigned myself to knowing that I couldn't do stuff like this for her. That she'd have to go without a lot of the things that other kids get. But now she has this, and it's beautiful. And you did it for her."

Understanding the sentiment, Noah said, "I did it for both of you." When she swiped at a tear, he added, "I'm serious. Get your ass on that slide and show her how it's done."

Carrie laughed, as he'd intended, and then grabbed Molly's toes when she swung forward. "You won't care about any other birthday presents after this one."

"Speaking of birthdays," he said, ready to get the asking over with. "My mom's is coming up this week. She's having a little party on Saturday, and I thought you might want to go." Quickly, he added, "You don't have to. My mom is kind of, well . . ." How to say this nicely? "She can be overwhelming when you don't know her." She could be overwhelming when you *did* know her, but Noah kept that fact to himself.

"Oh, um . . ." Carrie hedged.

"Forget about it. I'll go alone."

"I just don't know if I can get a babysitter."

"Why would you need a babysitter?"

"Because I have a baby?"

Noah gave Molly another push. "We'll take her with us."

"We will?"

"It's a family gathering at three in the afternoon. My mom doesn't let anyone smoke in her house, and she'd probably make us come back and get her if we didn't bring Molly."

"Oh." Carrie hugged her denim jacket tight over her chest. "Meeting the family, huh?"

"Yeah," he said. "You okay with that."

"Nervous," she replied. "I'm not going to lie. But sure. I'm okay with it."

"Good," Noah said, tweaking Molly's nose as she passed him. "Good."

∽

"Of all times for Lorelei to be out of town," Carrie said, examining the bakery options behind the glass.

"Yes," Haleigh said. "How dare she go on a honeymoon."

"You don't have to make me feel any stupider for saying that. But still. I'm meeting Noah's mother. I need Lorelei's cupcakes." Motioning toward the display, she said, "These might as well be sawdust next to hers."

Smiling at the woman behind the counter, Haleigh said, "She means that in the nicest way," before dragging Carrie down to the bread display. "I told you to ask Rosie. Where do you think Lorelei got all those recipes?"

"If I do that, I have to tell her why I need them, and we both know how that would go. She'd have a wedding announcement in the paper within a week."

"Lorelei does come by her hopeless romantic streak honestly. Though she'd never admit to having one at all."

Carrie checked her shopping list. "She might now that she's officially settled into her happily ever after."

"That really doesn't bother you, does it?"

"I need bananas," she replied, turning her buggy. "Not at all. If anything, it's a relief. She always should have been his wife."

Haleigh sidestepped a runaway toddler. "That's very mature of you."

"I spent a lot of years being immature about that situation. Didn't make me or Spencer very happy."

"And now look at you. He's blissfully married to the love of his life, and you're about to meet a potential mother-in-law."

Anxiety braided up her spine. "Don't call her that."

"I admit, it's early." Rolling an apple in her hand, she added, "But anytime a guy takes you home to his mother it's a big deal."

"If you recall, I've had two mothers-in-law already, and neither of them liked me." Carrie picked up a bunch of bananas and noticed another shopper doing the same. "Spencer's mother never said anything nice to me, though she was also never sober, so maybe it was the liquor talking." As the woman beside her reached for another bunch, the sleeve of her sweater rode up, revealing familiar finger-shaped bruises. "Patch's mother never thought I was good enough for her precious boy and had no problem telling me so."

"I do not understand that," Haleigh replied. "It isn't as if you're some obnoxious woman assaulting people with cheap perfume and cursing like a trucker with two days to make a three-day haul."

Staring at her friend, Carrie said, "You're starting to talk like Cooper."

"That *was* something he'd say, huh? The analogy still works." She ripped a plastic bag off the roll to her left and started filling it with apples. "There is no reason anyone shouldn't like you."

"Maybe my luck will change with this one." Carrie reached for the same bunch as the woman beside her did, and their hands bumped. "I'm so sorry," she said, turning to see a tiny scab at the corner of the woman's mouth. "Are you okay?"

"I'm fine," the stranger said, covering the split lip as she threw a random bunch in her basket and hurried away.

Watching her rush off, Haleigh said, "What spooked her?"

"She must be in a hurry," Carrie guessed, seeing no need to embarrass the woman by telling the truth. "I'd better go back and pick a dessert. The pies are good here, aren't they?"

"They aren't Lorelei's, but . . ."

"You're hysterical," she said, still thinking about the woman at the bananas.

If the shelter were open, Carrie would have slipped her a card. Provided her an alternative. A way out. But Safe Haven wasn't set to open for another six weeks. By then, this woman could be in the hospital. Or worse. Noah said the renovations to the camp were going well. Maybe he could speed things up and get the doors open sooner. She made a note to ask him on the way to the party.

Chapter 17

Noah's sweaty palms left damp spots on the steering wheel. For safety reasons, they'd brought Carrie's car, which he'd had to cram himself into. His truck was an older model and not safe for the car seat. Carrie had offered to drive, but he'd stared at her as if she'd suggested they snip off his balls on the way, and she tossed over the keys.

They were both tense, if the silence on the trip was any indication. He didn't know what Carrie was worried about, but Noah kept telling himself all the reasons Ma was sure to love her. For one, she was the total opposite of every other woman he'd ever brought home. In high school, he'd gone for brash and mouthy. Hell, after high school hadn't been much different. Felicia, his short-lived fiancée, had been the epitome of loud, cocky, and hotheaded. But Carrie was none of those things. Something his mother would likely be relieved to see.

Carrie's reaction to his family was the real concern. They were big. Affectionate. And exhausting. If she decided that being with him wasn't worth dealing with the gale-force winds of the Winchesters, Noah would lose the best thing he'd ever found. Besides giving him something to live for, she also kept the demons at bay. Without Carrie in his life, he feared the nightmares would return, stronger than before.

"This is it," he said, breaking the silence as he pulled down the drive of the old Victorian he'd grown up in.

"There are a lot of cars," Carrie pointed out. "I thought you said a little party?"

Counting eight cars and trucks scattered through the front yard, Noah should have known his mother had skirted the truth. "That's what she'd called it. We don't have to stay long."

"Noah, this is your mother's birthday party. She's barely seen you in years. We aren't leaving early."

"Are you sure you want to do this?" he asked, car still running. "I can take you guys home and come back."

Balancing a pie on her lap, Carrie said, "She isn't going to like me, is she? That's why you don't want me to go in."

"Don't be crazy. She's going to love you."

"Mothers never love me."

Now she was messing with him. "What are you talking about?"

She shook her head while holding up two fingers. "I've had *two* husbands, and neither of their mothers liked me, let alone loved me. I'm oh for two. This could be strike three."

Swinging his arm behind her seat, he turned to face her. "I don't know anything about your ex's mom, but Althea was never going to like anyone that Patch brought home. He could have married a doctor with a law degree and she'd have found something wrong with the woman."

"That doesn't make me feel any better," she said. "You're the only son, aren't you? I'm never going to be good enough for you, either. I've been married twice. I've never gone to college. I'm a single mother. Strikes all over the place."

"Did you sign up for Little League when I wasn't looking?"

"Don't make jokes. I'm freaking out here."

Molly fussed in the back, demanding to know why they were sitting still, but she was still stuck in her contraption.

"If anything," Noah said, cutting the engine, "it'll be you not liking my mother. She takes getting used to. And I'm talking several years before adjusting to the volume of her voice alone. But we aren't going to find out either way if we don't get out of this car." He held out his hand. "You with me?"

Carrie blew out a breath and twined her fingers through his. "Let's do this."

Noah kissed her knuckles before letting go to climb out. She carried the pie and diaper bag while Noah handled Molly. Halfway to the door, he spotted a burgundy Camaro.

"Shit."

"What?" she asked.

"Nothing," he said, hoping there was more than one burgundy Camaro in Ardent Springs.

Carrie's head spun with names and faces, and her jacket smelled like roses dipped in lavender thanks to several older women who'd skipped the simple handshake and come right in for a suffocating hug. Noah carrying Molly stirred the female guests into a frenzy, and she feared if one more person pinched her child's cheek she would snap before ever meeting his mother.

The large dining room to the left of the foyer presented countless offerings, including no fewer than four pies. Carrie added hers to the bunch, realizing right away that she'd brought the only store-bought version. Damn Lorelei and her flipping honeymoon.

"My mom is back in the kitchen," Noah whispered in her ear. "Smile and nod, but whatever you do, keep walking."

Happy to follow that order, Carrie locked her teeth and put her feet into motion. A heavyset woman Noah called Aunt Francine waylaid them right as they were set to pass through the doorway to the kitchen, but like a pro, he wedged them past the blockade to reach the bright florescent lights of their destination.

"Hallelujah! There's my boy!" boomed a voice that scared Molly into leaping for her mother. The woman who threw her arms around Noah's neck stood barely an inch shorter than him, and she was nearly as wide. Not heavy, but wide. Like a linebacker or a school bus. "When are you going to get rid of this rodent on your face?" she asked, tugging on his beard.

"When I feel like it, Ma." Taking Carrie's hand, he gave a squeeze as he said, "This is Carrie and her daughter, Molly. Carrie, this is my mother, Lydia Winchester."

"Oh," the older woman said in a much more tolerable tone. "Did I scare her?"

The loud voice could scare anyone, but Noah hadn't mentioned the sheer force of his mother's personality. Less destructive than a tornado, or so Carrie hoped, meeting this woman was just as daunting as seeing a funnel approach in the distance. Thankfully, her caring eyes exuded a genuine warmth that soothed Carrie's earlier fears.

Patting her daughter's back, Carrie said, "She's a little overwhelmed. I'm afraid we aren't used to this many people." Which wasn't true, since more people attended Sunday services than were in this house. But then the weekly congregation rarely tried to talk all at once.

"Let's go onto the back porch," Lydia said, leading the way through a side door. "Move, y'all. This child needs room to breathe."

To Carrie's relief, they stepped onto an empty screened-in porch with beautiful white wicker furniture and a wind chime in the corner playing a deep, soothing melody.

"There," Lydia said. "Much better." She spoke like a normal person while motioning toward a pillow-covered love seat. "Noah, get your girl something to drink while I get to know her." The quiet loosened Molly's grip on her mother's neck enough for her to peek at their hostess. "Oh, baby, you look like your daddy," Lydia said.

"Yes, she does," Carrie agreed. There would never be any denying Molly's parentage. "Your home is beautiful."

"It's even better without all these people. You'll have to come back another day and let me give you a full tour."

Noah hovered beside them, drawing his mother's glare. "Didn't I give you a chore to do?"

"You okay?" he asked Carrie.

She nodded. "We're fine." And thankfully, she meant the words.

Without another word, he disappeared into the kitchen.

"Well, butter my butt and call me a biscuit. I've never seen my boy dote on a woman like that."

"He's very caring," she said, unsure if the doting was a good or bad thing in his mother's eyes. "Molly loves him."

"I'm not surprised. He was always great with kids." Lydia tickled Molly's side, and the baby grabbed her finger. "For a long time I wondered if I'd ever get grandchildren out of him. Sometimes I thought he stayed single just to spite me."

Jumping to his defense, Carrie said, "I don't think his military career gave him much time to date."

Shifting her gaze from Molly's face to Carrie's, the older woman smiled. "I like you already."

"Really?" she said, unable to keep the shock from her voice.

"Why are you so surprised?"

Unable to lie to this woman, she said, "I don't have a great track record with the mothers of the men I've been involved with."

Lydia waved off her words, revealing perfectly manicured blood-red nails. "Althea always was too hoity-toity for her own good. Thought that boy of hers was the cat's meow when he was little more than a lazy hound dog collecting fleas under the porch." Carrie felt no urge whatsoever to defend her deceased husband or his mother, so she held her tongue. "I worried about Noah being out on the farm by himself. He didn't come back the same, you know."

"Yes. I know."

"That's why I sold you that land. Not because I thought for one minute all *this* would develop," she clarified, "but so he wouldn't be alone. The protective instinct is strong in that boy, and Noah never could have lived next to a pretty young woman and her adorable little girl without wanting to make sure they were okay. That you were a link to Patch, worthless as he may have been, was just a bonus."

Stunned by the revelation, Carrie said, "You knew more than a year ago that Noah planned to live on the farm?"

"He always loved that place. The quiet. The space. The good memories."

To think, she'd assumed their close proximity had happened by chance. When all along, a caring mother had been looking out for her son.

"I hope you don't mind my conniving," she said. "It seems to have worked out."

Relaxing for the first time in two days, Carrie said, "I don't mind at all."

"Good." Lydia tapped two fingers on Molly's knee. "You're too cute for words, darlin'."

As if recognizing another potential conquest, the baby reached for the stranger with open arms. The older woman's eyes moistened with emotion, and Carrie sent up a prayer of thanks that Lydia Winchester loved her son enough to put him in Carrie's path.

During his mission to get the drinks, Noah made a pass through the dining room to load a plate with anything he thought Carrie and Molly might like to nibble on. With a stuffed mushroom hovering halfway to its destination, Noah spotted the Camaro owner. Why in the hell had his mother invited Kyra? Grabbing two napkins, he tried to duck out before she saw him, but Kyra cut him off at the doorway to the kitchen.

"I can't believe you brought her," she hissed, heedless of who overheard.

"Get out of my way, Kyra."

"I don't get it. Does the little-miss-innocent thing do it for you?" Stealing an olive from his plate, she added, "Because I can do that. Hell, I'll put on the schoolgirl uniform and go all out."

Embarrassed for her, Noah tried to be patient. "Why are you so desperate for attention?"

"I go after what I want," she said. "Does that intimidate you? Maybe the truth is that you can't handle me and you know it. That's why you settle for the meek little mouse when you could have all of this." Leaning forward, she pressed her breasts against his arm.

"Have a little respect. If not for yourself, then think about Lenny." Noah stepped around her, but Kyra didn't give up.

"I told you. Lenny lets me do what I want."

"Lenny doesn't let you do anything," he snapped, dragging her to the back corner of the kitchen. "You married a nice guy with earning potential who would never tell you no. You're spoiled and you're selfish, and if you cared about the poor sap at all, you'd stop embarrassing him. Now I'm telling you for the last time, I'm not interested. And if you dare to say one word to Carrie while we're here, I'll make sure your scam of a marriage ends quick. You got me?"

Heavily lined eyes narrowed to slits. "She'll make you miserable just like she made Patch miserable. I hope you both burn in hell."

Though he'd tried to keep his voice down, they'd still garnered an audience, which Kyra stormed through on her way out of the kitchen. Furious with himself for letting her get to him, Noah snagged two bottles of water from the fridge and returned to the porch. To his utter amazement, he found his tearful mother holding a laughing baby in the air.

"That's my job," he said, setting the plate and drinks on the table next to Carrie before reaching for Molly. "What's all this misty-eyed crap? You didn't even cry when I left for boot camp."

"I'm getting sentimental in my old age," his mother said. "Give me a break."

Noah tucked Molly against his side, and the smell hit him immediately. "Whoa. Tell Mommy your bottom needs some attention."

Carrie rose to her feet. "I'd better take her out to the car and change her."

"Don't be silly," Lydia said. "Use the bedroom on the left at the top of the stairs. You can't miss it."

"Thank you," she said. "We'll be right back."

Before she could walk away, Noah placed a hard kiss on her lips.

"What was that for?" Carrie asked.

"Just hadn't done it for a while," he replied, gratitude welling in his chest. A bashful smile teased her lips as she walked away.

"Looks like I'm not the only one getting sappy with age," Ma said once Carrie was out of sight.

Ignoring the comment, he said, "Why is Kyra Persimmon here?"

"Lenny is my accountant," Lydia answered. "And he's your friend, so I invited him. Unfortunately, that means the petulant child comes along, too."

"She was always a brat, but I thought she'd grow out of it."

Lydia snorted. "She grew into that body and brought the brat with her. Poor Lenny is the laughingstock of Ardent Springs, but I hold out hope that he'll wake up and send her packing eventually." Tapping the seat next to her, she said, "Now, tell me, is this as serious as it looks?"

Noah settled onto the creaking wicker. "We're still early in, but yeah."

"You look better than when you first came home," she observed. "More peaceful."

"That's Carrie's doing," he said, cutting his eyes to the towering pines outside. "She believes I can get better in time."

Ma had always been good at reading between the lines. "But you don't."

Tapping his leg, he gave her a half smile. "I want to. That's better than a few months ago."

"Good. And not that you care, but I like her. She's a breath of fresh air compared to what you've dragged into this house before."

"They weren't all bad," he defended. Eyes similar to his own stared through his skull. "You're right." Noah opened a bottle of water. "I don't know what I was thinking back then."

"Oh, I know what you were thinking," she said, lifting a small meatball off the plate. "And what you were thinking with."

His mother's booming laughter shattered the serenity of the porch. She always had enjoyed cracking herself up.

Chapter 18

"You did a number on that one, baby," Carrie said, holding her breath as she closed up the dirty diaper. "Oh no you don't." She caught the fleeing child before Molly hurled herself off the side of the bed. "Let's go back down and see Lydia. I bet they'll cut the cake soon."

"She's getting big," came a voice from behind her, startling Carrie.

Turning, she found Kyra Farmer—now Persimmon, she reminded herself—standing in the doorway.

"What are you doing here?"

The younger woman ignored the question. "The squirt looks exactly like Patch. You'll never be able to deny who her father is. At least that's something."

"We should go." Carrie stepped forward, but Kyra blocked the exit.

"Mama deserves to see her grandbaby."

"I'm not having this conversation with you. Let me by."

Kyra touched the hair above Molly's ear. "She's a Farmer. She's one of us."

Temper rising, Carrie said, "She'll never be one of you. Ever."

"You're such a bitch. Patch should have left your ass years ago."

"I wish he would have." Pushing through, she added, "Noah will be looking for us."

"You think you have him wrapped around your finger, don't you?"

Ignoring the taunt, Carrie kept moving. Footsteps echoed on the hardwood as the hateful girl followed.

"He'll get tired of you soon."

"Go to hell, Kyra."

"I've already fucked Noah once," she snarled, lip curled in rage as she beat Carrie to the steps. "He'll come back for more. They always come back for more."

Refusing to believe the lie, Carrie kept her voice even. "Get out of my way. Now."

"It's a good thing that kitchen table of his is sturdy," she said. "You know the one, right? With the yellow top and ugly red chairs?"

The color drained from Carrie's face.

"Oh, you believe me now, don't you? Noah has a hearty appetite. And you will *never* be enough for him."

Pointed heels clicked down the stairs as Kyra disappeared into the party without a backward glance. Knees weak, Carrie slowly sank down to sit on the top step. Drums beat in her ears as a headache raged to life behind her temples.

Kyra had to be lying. Noah wouldn't do that. He wasn't that guy. But how else could she have described the table? The night they'd talked about Molly seeing Patch's family, he said he'd run into Kyra. Right. Ran into her naked in his kitchen.

Unaware of how she'd gotten down the stairs, Carrie found herself standing on the edge of the crowd as someone carried a yellow cake into the dining room. The gathering broke into song, but she didn't join in. She didn't cheer when the candles went out. Or get in line to taste the main dessert. Carrie didn't do any of those things. Instead, she remained in the foyer, staring straight ahead but seeing nothing. Her body felt heavy. As if someone had filled her veins with cement.

She didn't move for several minutes until Noah appeared in front of her.

Snapping his fingers, he said, "Hello? Anyone in there?"

Carrie blinked, and when Noah reached for Molly, she jerked the child away.

"I want to go home."

"Now? Ma hasn't opened her—"

"Yes," she interrupted. "I want to go now."

Noah put his hand on the small of her back, but she stepped out of reach.

"Babe, what's wrong?"

"I want to go home," she repeated.

Tears threatened to shatter her control. Not tears of sadness, but tears of rage. She'd picked the wrong man. Again.

"Okay," he said, tone soothing as if he were dealing with a hysterical child. "Let's tell Ma that we're leaving."

Carrie shook her head. "You tell her. We'll be in the car."

"Hold on," Noah said. "We can leave together."

But Carrie was already out the door.

Noah tried several times to get Carrie to talk to him, but she wouldn't stop staring out the damn window. He touched her knee, and she smacked his hand away. By the time they reached the main road to the farm, his patience had worn thin. What the hell was he supposed to do if she wouldn't tell him what the problem was? And what could have happened between the time she left him on the porch and when she came back downstairs.

The answer was obvious.

Kyra.

The little menace must have found Carrie alone upstairs. But what did she say? If she pulled that shit about Carrie being the reason Patch was dead, Noah would strangle her himself. Whatever it was, he wasn't about to drag the answer out of Carrie with Molly nodding off in the backseat. The minute he parked in front of the trailer, Carrie burst out of the car. The same time she opened the back door on her side, Noah opened the opposite one on his.

"I'll carry her in," he said.

"I'll get her," she replied.

"Carrie," he said, his voice low. "I get that you're pissed. Go open the door and I'll take her in. Then we'll talk."

"I don't want to talk," she snapped, but she did climb out of the car and let him get the baby.

Noah got Molly into the crib and removed her tiny shoes without waking her up. Stepping into the living room, he found Carrie standing with her arms crossed at the end of the coffee table. Wilson meowed near the empty bowl in the kitchen, but his owner ignored him.

"Let's go outside," Noah said, reaching for her hand.

"Don't touch me," she said, stepping back. "You need to go home."

"I'm not going home until I find out what Kyra said to you."

Blue eyes shot up. "How do you know I talked to Kyra?"

Noah ran a hand through his hair, struggling for patience.

"Just come outside so we don't wake the baby."

Lips pinched, Carrie stormed onto the porch.

"Do you want to sit?" he asked.

Carrie shook her head.

"Fine. What did Kyra say?"

"You know so much, you tell me."

"This isn't a game, Carrie."

"Are you sure?" she said, a scary smirk on her face. "Maybe this was a game all along. Cuddle up to the widow next door. Make her think you care. That she's *special*. And then bang your dead best friend's little sister on your kitchen table so the tramp would see how it feels to be humiliated. Give her a taste of her own medicine, right? Cheat on the cheater."

Breathing deeply to control his reaction, Noah locked his hands at his sides. "Is that what she told you? That we had sex on my kitchen table?"

"You know," Carrie said, mimicking Kyra's nasally twang, "the yellow one with the red chairs. How else would she know that, Noah?" Waving her hands in the air, she shook her head. "Forget I asked. This is over."

"This is not over," Noah growled. "Kyra showed up at my house the day of the bachelorette party. She brought one of Althea's pies and made no secret that I was welcome to a lot more than dessert."

"I don't want to hear this," Carrie said.

"I kicked her out," he continued. "But she made it as far as the kitchen, where she set the pie on the table. *That's* how she knows what my stupid table looks like."

"Why would she lie?"

"Have you *met* her?" Noah asked. "I saw her at the party when I left you with Mom to get the drinks. She said she didn't get how I could want you over her, and I snapped. I told her I would never want her and that if she dared to talk to you, I'd make sure Lenny grew a nut and left her ass." Noah ran a hand through his hair as he stalked from side to side. "I should have known that she'd pull something like this anyway."

Staring at the floor, Carrie said, "So you didn't have sex with her?"

Wanting so badly to hit something, Noah said, "Even if I'd never met you, I would not have sex with Patch's little sister. Not only is she practically a child, she's married. To one of my friends. I'm a lot of things, Carrie, but I'm not . . . that."

Slamming her hands into her hair, she dropped onto the glider. "I didn't believe her until she described the table. I knew she had to be lying, but I fell for it anyway."

Noah crossed the porch to sit beside her, but Carrie bolted up as soon as his ass hit the bench.

"I ruined your mother's birthday party. I ruined us. All because of that malicious woman. I'm such an idiot."

"You didn't ruin anything," he assured her, but the rant continued.

"I insulted *you*. I made a fool of myself," she said, pounding her chest. "What is wrong with me?"

Taking her by the shoulders, he said, "Look at me, baby. Calm down and look at me."

Shoulders heavy with defeat, she lifted her eyes.

"The only way Kyra wins here is if we let her. Right?" Carrie blinked, but she nodded. "I'm not letting that happen. How about you?"

"Two minutes ago, I thought the worst of you."

"I thought the worst of me for the last year," he said.

By some miracle, she laughed. "I've screwed up so many times." Carrie caressed his cheek. "I want to do something right for a change."

Drunk on relief and something a hell of a lot bigger, Noah said, "This is right, baby. You and me against the world. You can't get more right than that."

"Remind me to thank your mother the next time I see her," she said, wrapping her arms around his middle.

"Thank her for what?" he asked with a chuckle.

"For making all my hopes and dreams come true."

Noah didn't see what his mom had to do with that, but he didn't say so. Instead, he held his girl tight to his chest and sent off his own thanks to whatever higher power had brought her to him.

∽

Hours after nearly destroying the best thing that had ever happened to her, Carrie drifted off to sleep secure in the arms of the man she loved. They hadn't intended to fall asleep on the couch, but the emotional upheaval of the afternoon paired with lack of sleep the night before had done her in. And she couldn't think of a better place to lay her head than over Noah's heart.

Because he never slept a full night in her bed, she remained clueless to the nightmares. Until this night.

Ripped from a sound sleep, Carrie found herself flying through the air to land hard on her side between the couch and the coffee table. Feeling as if she'd been hit by a train, she slowly rolled onto her bottom and discovered Noah sitting straight up on the couch, covered in sweat, and breathing like a man who'd been running for his life. His eyes were open, but he wasn't behind them. Wherever his brain still lingered, she knew that putting herself within reach would be a bad idea.

Crab crawling backward, she said, "Noah? Honey? You're okay."

No reaction.

"Noah, it's Carrie. Wake up now. It's just a dream."

His chest still heaved, but his breathing slowed. Brown eyes returned to normal before he dropped his head in his hands and wiped his face.

"Carrie?" he said, searching the area with panic in his voice.

"I'm okay," she said, rolling to her feet, ignoring the pain that shot through her hip. "I'm right here. We're both okay."

"You weren't," Noah said, shaking his head. "Some guy had you. I couldn't get out. I couldn't open the damn door."

She held his face so he could look into her eyes. "No one has me, baby. I'm right here, and I'm fine."

He crushed her against him, forcing her to put weight on the injured hip. When she yipped, he said, "What happened? You're hurt. I hurt you."

"No. I promise, you didn't hurt me. I just fell off the couch."

Unconvinced, he ran his hands over her arms. "Where does it hurt?"

"Nothing hurts," she replied before shifting to the right and failing to smother the cry of pain.

"Dammit. That isn't nothing."

Carrie rose to her feet and tested the joint. "I can put weight on it. See?" She bounced on one leg pain-free. "I might have a bruise from where I hit the floor, but I've done worse tripping over my own feet."

"I hate these goddamn things." He set his feet on the floor and shoved the hair out of his face. "I haven't had that one in weeks."

Seizing the opening, Carrie curled up beside him, careful to keep her weight on the opposite side. "How often do you have nightmares?" she asked.

Noah shook his head. "Used to be every night. Lately it's been maybe two a week. Less disturbing than before."

"Lately as in the last six months, or six days?"

"Since we got together," he replied, taking her hand. "But the one with you and Molly snuck up on me."

Surprised, she said, "Molly is in the dream?"

"Nightmare," he corrected. "Yeah. Skipping the details, you're both in danger and I can see it, but I can't get to you."

Out of her depth, Carrie dug for clues that might help get rid of the dream. "You said a man had me. Who was it?"

He let out a long, slow breath. "I can't see his face. Just a figure. But I don't think that part matters."

"No, I guess not." They both knew that figure represented Patch, even if Noah didn't admit as much. "What happens in the other ones? The ones that Molly and I aren't in?"

"The other nightmares are stuff that happened during my time overseas."

She could only imagine the horror he'd witnessed, but she would never ask for details. "And you say they've gotten less frequent? That's a good thing, right?"

"Yeah, babe. That's a good thing." Noah rose to his feet. "I'd better get home and let you sleep."

Worrying about him in the farmhouse all alone would keep her up the rest of the night.

"Why don't you stay?"

He turned her way. "What about Molly? What if she wakes up?"

Carrie smiled. "I don't think she'd mind finding her favorite person spending the night."

Pulling her off the couch, he said, "Are you sure? I don't want to mess Molly up."

Tucking a caramel lock behind his ear, she said, "Go get your toothbrush, Mr. Winchester. I'll be waiting when you get back." Lifting her into a kiss, Noah squeezed her hips, drawing another painful grunt. "I may be sitting on a frozen bag of peas," she moaned, "but I'll be waiting."

Noah kissed her again, his touch carefully gentle. When they parted, he looked into her eyes. "I love you, Carrie."

Breath catching in her throat, she nodded. "I love you, too. Now hurry back so I can show you how much."

Chapter 19

Three days later, Carrie continued to float several feet off the ground. They'd spent the weekend creating Molly's first Halloween costume, which turned into quite the debate. Two weeks shy of eleven months old, her daughter would never remember what she wore, nor would she care about the candy. Not that Carrie wouldn't let her try a sweet or two, but collecting an entire bag of nothing but sugar seemed unnecessary.

Noah disagreed. And in the end, he'd won the argument.

The Ardent Springs downtown merchants ran a trick-or-treating event every year with most of the stores on Main Street staying open later than usual to hand out candy. Snow's Curiosity Shop would undoubtedly be a favorite this season, since Lorelei planned to give away tiny bags of her most popular cookies. When Noah picked up that tidbit, he'd insisted they start the evening right there.

"Lorelei, wait until you see this costume." Carrie rocked her desk chair while holding the cell phone to her ear. "I can't believe he found a leather jacket small enough to fit her. She even has her own transportation. Noah insisted that every biker needs a bike, so he painted her tricycle black and put a horn on it."

"That man is wrapped around her finger," Lorelei said.

And Carrie was wrapped around his. Truth be told, he'd won the argument by playing dirty, gaining her surrender seconds before launching her into a mind-numbing orgasm.

"We've had two cuties in here already today," Lorelei said. "A ladybug and a boy wizard. And Snow has gone all-out, as usual. This year she's a flapper. I think she just wanted a reason to wear her boa again."

"Mine is still sitting on Noah's bedroom floor."

"Spencer cut mine in half, and we put it to good use."

"Did not need to know that." Carrie checked the clock. "I'd better get moving. I'm leaving early to pick up Molly. I'll change her at the day care, and Noah is meeting us at your place with the trike. Hopefully, we'll get a couple of blocks down before she gets tired and cranky."

"You guys have turned into a little family, haven't you?"

"I guess we have," she replied. Once upon a time, the word *family* triggered ugly memories for Carrie. To actually smile when hearing it now was proof of how much her life had changed. "I can't remember ever being this happy."

"Maybe you'll be the next one going on a honeymoon." Carrie couldn't imagine her life without Noah, but she wasn't ready to go dress shopping either. "Oh," Lorelei added, "I have a present for Miss Molly."

"You don't buy gifts for other people when you're on your honeymoon," Carrie scolded.

"Says who?"

Excellent question. "I don't know. I'm sure it's a rule somewhere."

"So I broke a rule. Not the first time, and it won't be the last."

The office phone rang, and Noah's cell number showed in the display. "Lor, I've got to go. Noah is calling on my desk phone."

"Is that how it's going to be now? Drop the rest of us like a hot potato as soon as your hunk of burning love snaps his fingers?"

"I'm going, Lorelei. I'll see you tonight." Carrie ended one call and answered the other. "Hey there."

"Do you know where Mike is?" Noah asked.

Not the romantic greeting she'd hoped for. "He's with an inspector over at the church project."

"That explains why he isn't answering his phone. We have a problem out here."

Carrie straightened. "What problem?"

"This isn't good."

"Noah, tell me what's going on."

A sigh echoed down the line, and Carrie could almost see him running a hand through his hair. "The plumber started working on the new bathrooms and discovered that the pipe leading out to the septic tank is disintegrated. As far as we can tell, the entire line, start to finish, needs to be replaced."

So they needed to replace one pipe. That didn't sound so bad. "Okay. Then put a new one in."

"It isn't that simple. We'll have to break through the floor in every room, remove and replace the pipe, and then repair the floor. On top of that, it's safe to assume the septic tank isn't any good either."

"The shelter has to have a septic system. The city doesn't service out that far."

"I know that, hon, but these repairs aren't in your budget or the schedule. Three days of rain last week already put us behind. Adding these repairs means we're looking at a new end date of maybe middle of December. And that's *if* everything goes smoothly from here on out."

A delay was unacceptable.

"Noah, the shelter opens on December first."

"Not now it doesn't."

Frustration tightened her jaw. "I can't go to the board and tell them that we aren't opening on time because of one pipe."

"We aren't talking a little water line to a faucet here. This puppy runs the full length of the building, and it's rotted through." Noah's voice was muffled as he spoke to someone in the room with him.

"I can't believe this," she said, frantically searching for a way to get the project back on track.

"I need approval before we start ripping through the floors," Noah said. "The plumber estimates the cost around thirty-five hundred. Six grand if the tank is bad. Is your board willing to cough up that money to get this done?"

Oh God, this meant she had to call Meredith.

"I have no idea, but I'll find out. And I'll talk to Mike about adding to the crew to get the job done on time."

"Good luck with that," he said, "but you'd be looking at additional cost for that as well. These guys don't work for free."

"Noah, you have to make this work. We need that shelter open on the original date."

"Carrie, I'm not a freaking magician. What do you want me to do?"

"I don't know," she snapped. "You're the guy in charge, and you have a deadline to hit, so figure it out."

Though he'd clearly dropped the phone away from his ear, Carrie still heard the expletive. "Have Mike call me," he barked before breaking the connection.

Staring at the receiver in her hand, Carrie couldn't believe he'd hung up on her. How did he not understand the importance of getting the shelter up and running as soon as possible? There were women suffering who needed this resource. Needed it now, not maybe by Christmas, or maybe after the first of the year. She remembered the skittish woman in the grocery store and nearly ground her teeth.

At the same time, a tiny voice in her brain pointed out that snapping at Noah wouldn't solve anything. He hadn't taken a hammer to that stupid pipe, and as he said, he wasn't a magician, or a miracle worker. He was a guy doing the best he could who didn't need his girlfriend making his life miserable.

She owed him an apology, but it would have to wait.

It was already past the time she'd planned to leave, so Carrie shut down her computer and grabbed her purse. On her way to the car, she sent Mike a 911 text to call Noah right away. After buckling her seat belt, she took a deep breath, pondering her next move. She could call Meredith and explain the situation. Or she could drive nails into her eyeballs, which sounded slightly less torturous.

Choice made, she scrolled through her contacts until she found the number she wanted.

∽

By the time his boss's name appeared on his phone, Noah had calmed down enough not to rip anyone's head off. He hadn't busted the damn pipe, and he wasn't going to push his crew to work twelve-hour days to hit what was already an unrealistic deadline.

"What's going on out there?" Mike asked. "Do we have an injury?"

Only Noah's sanity, but that had been thin to begin with.

"The cast iron under this building is practically compost. We have to replace the whole thing."

"Damn," floated through the line. "How much are we talking?"

"Estimate is around thirty-five hundred, but that's only parts and labor to run the new pipe under the building. Throw in a new septic tank, since the current one is probably shot, and you're up to six grand. Ballpark, of course."

"Meredith isn't going to take that well."

Frustrated and annoyed, Noah said, "You need to deal with her *and* Carrie. This December one deadline isn't going to happen. Carrie seems to think I can pull a miracle out of my ass, and you don't pay me enough to get bitched at for something that's out of my control."

"Are you saying Carrie chewed you out?" Mike asked.

"She got pissed when I told her we'd have to push back the open date."

"Carrie? Our Carrie?"

Ignoring what he considered a stupid question, Noah said, "We're tapping out for today. Let me know by morning if we're cleared to start on the pipe."

"They'll have to pay for it or they don't get a shelter," Mike said. "Consider this your approval and get back at it first thing in the morning."

"Whatever you say, boss." Noah slid the phone into his back pocket and trudged through the building sending guys home. If he hurried, he could still meet Carrie before the Halloween stuff started. Her copping an attitude didn't mean Molly would collect her candy with only half a costume.

When he made the turn from Fifth onto Main, he found the sidewalks flooded with everything from princesses to zombies. Traffic crawled, so he took the first left and found a spot along the curb on Fourth Avenue North. Hauling the mini-Harley from the back of the truck, he walked down to the shop on the corner, where they'd agreed to meet. Carrie and Molly weren't outside, so he stepped through the entrance and instantly felt out of place.

What wasn't breakable was bright pink or yellow, and the tables had been placed so close together he had to turn sideways to keep from knocking them over. A tablecloth caught on a back wheel of the trike and nearly sent an entire set of dishes crashing to the floor. Between all the accidents waiting to happen and the people milling about, Noah's palms grew clammy as his heart rate kicked up. If he didn't spot Carrie in the next three seconds, he'd make his way back outside and call her.

"Noah?" said the woman behind the counter.

Terri Osburn

"Hey there," he said, recognizing the maid of honor from the wedding, though the 1920s getup nearly threw him off.

"Happy Halloween. If you're looking for Carrie, she's in the cafe with Lorelei."

"Thanks," he said, attempting a relaxed smile, but doubting he'd pulled it off.

As he approached, Lorelei spotted him first, since Carrie had her back to the store.

"Looks like she'll have her motorbike after all," she said.

Molly squealed at the sight of him as her mother turned around.

"You're here," she said.

Noah put the trike on the floor. "This is where you said to be."

"But I didn't think . . . I mean, after the phone call . . ."

"I said I'd be here."

"Right. I know."

Taking the baby, Lorelei said, "Why don't I take our little biker girl here and see what Snow has up at the counter. You two talk amongst yourselves."

Carrie looked as if she'd prefer Lorelei stay, but the other woman cut out quick.

Crossing her arms, she asked, "Did Mike call you?"

"Yep." Noah preferred not to bring business home.

"What did he say?"

"Ask him tomorrow."

"I'm asking you now."

"And I said ask him tomorrow." Didn't she understand? He didn't want to fight with her. He didn't want to let his mouth spout something that would screw up what they had. "We're off the clock, so let it go."

"I don't think you understand how important this shelter is," Carrie said.

"Is it more important than us?" he asked.

"What kind of a question is that?"

190

Noah made an extra effort to keep his voice low. "I told you when we started the construction that things always creep up. Always. You talking to me like a piece of shit doesn't change the reality. The job will take as long as it takes. If you can't get your panties out of a bunch and deal with that, I don't know what to tell you. But I didn't sign up to be your whipping boy."

Gaze dropping to his chin, she said, "I'm sorry. I shouldn't have gotten so upset with you."

He watched her close in on herself, practically shrinking before his eyes.

"Don't do that."

"Do what?"

"Act like I'm going to hit you."

Her face paled. "You wouldn't hit me."

"I know, but that fight-or-flight part of your brain hasn't gotten the message." Noah took her hands and pulled her toward one of the stools at the cookie counter. "You got frustrated and took it out on the messenger. It happens. People get mad, but that doesn't mean fists will fly. Not with me."

"I'm sorry," she said again.

"Don't—"

"I know. I know. I'm trying here, okay?" Carrie scraped dust off his jeans. "I have triggers just like you do, Noah. It's not something I'm proud of. But I really do owe you an apology for going off like that. So I'm sorry."

He tucked her head into his shoulder. "Apology accepted."

Her head rolled from side to side. "I just really want the shelter open." She pulled back and rested her hands on his thighs. "Not long ago, in the grocery store, a woman reached for some bananas and I saw the bruises. I know those bruises like I know my own name, Noah. She tugged her sleeve down when she caught me staring, and wouldn't make eye contact. I wanted to tell her that there was a place she could go. That she didn't have to stay with him. She didn't have to take another punch."

If Carrie was trying to break him open, she was doing a damn good job.

"We'll get there," he said. "In six weeks instead of four, but we'll get there."

Carrie swiped a tear off her cheek. "It breaks my heart, you know? I want to save them all."

Tipping up her chin, he said, "There's nothing wrong with that, baby. You'll have your shelter soon. Now what do you say we go get us some candy?"

"You mean get Molly some candy," she corrected with a hiccup.

"Sure." He took her hand, letting her lead the way through the store. "That's what I meant."

Chapter 20

While October had been unusually warm, November came in with an arctic blast. During the day, the sun made the crisp air almost bearable, but once the sun went down, which it would do much earlier once they turned the clocks back in a week, heavy coats were required.

Tuesday had not been Carrie's lucky day. She and Mike had discussed how to alert Meredith to the necessary budget increase, and because she'd called Haleigh the day before and scheduled a meeting between herself and the two Mitchner women for this evening, Mike took the easy way out and left the revelation to her.

The bad luck continued when it took her nearly five minutes to find a parking space at Lancelot's Restaurant, finally locating one in the high and yonder section of the lot. Hustling to the door, she cursed herself for not grabbing a scarf that morning. How had Mother Nature experienced such a change of heart overnight? They'd barely needed light jackets during trick-or-treating.

Shivering as she approached the hostess stand, Carrie said, "I'm with the Mitchner party."

"They're already seated," said the friendly teen. "I'll show you the way."

Lovely. Meredith hated to be kept waiting. Not the auspicious start she'd hoped for.

"Hey, Carrie," said Haleigh, rising from her chair to offer a quick hug. "She's in a good mood," she whispered in Carrie's ear. "Hallelujah."

"Sorry I'm late." Shrugging out of her coat, she hung it on her chair. "I couldn't find a parking space."

"There's a Ruby Restoration meeting," Haleigh reminded her.

"I should have remembered. That's the reason Lorelei couldn't watch Molly."

"Where is she then?" Meredith asked, speaking for the first time.

Clearing her throat, Carrie sat and spread a napkin across her lap. "Noah has her."

"Really?" the younger Mitchner said, before catching her friend's glaring message. "I mean, that's great. He's great with her." Haleigh stuck her nose in her menu. "I wonder what the specials are tonight?"

"Michael says Noah has the shelter project well in hand," Meredith drawled, examining her own menu. "I suppose I might have judged him a little too quickly."

Carrie and Haleigh exchanged a look that communicated every bit of shock and awe coursing through them both.

"About that," Carrie hedged. "We ran into a little snag."

"Maybe we should order our drinks first," Haleigh suggested, waving over a waiter. "Two waters and a pinot grigio," she said with a smile. "And keep the wine coming."

Meredith closed the menu. "Haleigh Rae, you don't need to ply me with wine to tell me whatever this little snag happens to be."

"So you don't want the wine?" the waiter asked.

"I didn't say that," she replied with an *are you an idiot?* glower. "I also want the baked tilapia with a side of mixed vegetables and a Caesar salad."

The poor boy shifted from foot to foot. "I'm sorry, but I'm not your waiter."

"Do you have a little notebook in your pocket?" she asked.

"Uh, yeah."

"Then I suggest you write this down and hand it to whomever is our waiter."

Carrie kept her head down, wishing for the first time ever that she'd acquired a taste for wine. Or whiskey.

"I'll have the baked chicken," Haleigh said, smart enough not to contradict her mother. "Broccoli and a house salad. Ranch please."

When Carrie didn't share her order, Haleigh kicked her under the table. "Oh. My turn. Sorry. I'll have the chicken as well. With corn and a Caesar."

As the waiter finished taking his notes, another server joined them. "Charlie, what are you doing? This is my table."

"He's taking our order since you were apparently busy elsewhere." Meredith handed the harried teen her menu. "Thank you for being so prompt, Charlie." Did she forget that Haleigh had motioned him over? "I trust that you'll make sure our orders are placed right away."

"Yes, ma'am," the youngster said, his voice cracking on the second word. "Here, Josh. Go place their orders." Head down, Charlie ditched his fellow server, leaving Josh staring after him.

Meredith tapped a manicured nail on the tabletop. "Ticktock, my boy. Your tip is dwindling." This is what Haleigh called a good mood? "Now, why am I here?" she said, turning on her tablemates.

Haleigh cleared her throat as she straightened her silverware. "An unforeseen problem was discovered under the shelter floors that will require additional funds for repair. This also means we can't open on our target date."

"What unforeseen problem?"

"The septic pipes have disintegrated," Haleigh answered. "The whole thing needs to be replaced."

"And the additional cost?" she asked, taking this much better than Carrie had feared.

"The estimate is six thousand," her daughter said, visibly bracing for the blowback.

Meredith didn't blow. She didn't even flinch. "That's less than we have in the contingency fund, so we're fine."

Leaning her elbows on the table, Haleigh said, "There's a contingency fund?"

"Elbows off," her mother admonished. "Of course there's a contingency fund. Projects like these are unpredictable. I would have been a fool to believe we wouldn't run into some sort of problem. I planned accordingly."

Life was just full of miracles these days.

"Okay then," Haleigh said, straightening the napkin in her lap. "I guess we don't have a problem after all."

"There's still the issue of the open date," Meredith reminded her. "What are we looking at now?"

"December sixteenth," Carrie offered. "Mike, Noah, and I believe that's a realistic target."

"Fine," Meredith said, once again taking the news in stride. "We'll hold off on the promotional materials for a few more weeks to be sure. Is there anything else?"

Carrie shook her head as Josh arrived with their drinks. "No, that's everything."

Topic dropped, Meredith once again turned her attention to the waiter. "Joshua, would it be possible to get our basket of bread before our meals arrive?"

As the server hurried off, Haleigh shot Carrie a relieved smile. Hopefully, Noah's night was going as well as theirs.

⟨∽⟩

"Molly, you're supposed to eat it, not wear it."

Noah had already pulled the munchkin's shirt off, since she kept smashing peas into the material instead of keeping them in her mouth. He assumed washing the green stains off her skin would be easier than getting them out of the cotton.

"Your mommy says you love these things." He waved the plastic container under his nose and cringed. "This explains the smell when they come out the other end."

In preparation for his first night flying solo with the little princess—whom he now considered renaming the holy terror—they'd relocated several necessities to his house, including a high chair, a bouncer contraption that hung in the doorway between the living room and the kitchen, a playpen, and the walker that had run over his toes so often in the last week that Noah longed for the day she took her first steps. Carrie had insisted they needed the deadly plastic contraption until then.

The only reason they were at his house instead of the trailer was the temperature outside. Carrie's windows were drafty as hell, and her heater worked only so well. The farmhouse might be ancient, but his grandmother had been a cold-natured woman who'd demanded that her husband insulate the thing to within an inch of its life. Which meant his humble abode remained warm and toasty no matter what Mother Nature whipped up outside.

Trying the airplane trick, Noah sent a cargo flight of peas careening toward Molly's mouth only to crash and burn. "Okay, you win," he said, crossing to the sink to run hot water. "We'll wipe you down and get back to our walking exercises."

His lack of furniture provided plenty of space for Molly to test her mobility without hurting herself. He'd moved the coffee table into Granny's old sewing room, eliminating the one danger near the couch.

By dinnertime she'd tiptoed from one end of the sofa to the other at least twenty times, each pass ending when she let go and landed on her bottom. It only took ten times for Noah to stop panicking and checking for injuries every time she fell.

While the water got warm, he searched the bag that seemed to have magical powers. Need a diaper? It's in there. Need teething medicine? It's in there. Need a new probe for the space station? Noah had no doubt it was in there.

The first thing he pulled out was a purple top covered in dark pink flowers. Testing the opening, it looked like something he could probably get over her head without breaking the child's neck. Next he found a lime-green pair of pants. Worked for him. Five minutes later, he had a relatively clean baby dusting his hardwood with her ugly green pants.

"Don't let gravity win this time, Mol," he said, grabbing the stack of mail from the counter and following her. "You can do this."

Noah plopped down on the couch and let the little one climb up his leg. Keeping one eye on her, he surveyed the envelopes and found another piece from the VA. Tossing the ads and utility bills aside, he opened the letter to find that he had until the end of the month to enroll in the new PTSD study.

"Because that's what I want for Christmas. A giant pile of side effects topped with a bow of disappointment."

The sound of the screen door slipping open caught his attention, and Noah managed to shove the letter down into the couch before Carrie stepped into the house.

"Hey," she said, looking a lot happier than he'd expect after spending time with Meredith Mitchner. "Molly, honey, what are you wearing?"

"She's wearing clothes," Noah answered, pointing out the obvious while Carrie wiggled out of her coat. "That's what you had in the bag."

Carrie laughed. "Each of those pieces has another half, and that is not it. Did she eat?"

Sort of answering the question, he said, "There's only half a thing of peas left." Which was technically true.

"Where's the other half?" the knowing mother queried, with one brow riding high.

"Hard to say. Her shirt," he confessed. "The tray. The floor. Best guess, at least a quarter of it stayed in her mouth."

"A quarter is an amazing feat for your first try." Carrie hung her jacket on the coat tree and crossed to the couch. Bending to drop a kiss on his lips, she said, "Hi."

"Hi yourself. You're in a good mood considering who you were with."

"You aren't going to believe how well that went." She took the other end of the couch since Molly blocked the middle cushion. "Not only did Meredith admit that she might have judged you too quickly—her words—but back when she created the renovation budget, she added a contingency fund for any unforeseen expenses. Like replacing a useless septic system."

"I'll be damned," he mumbled.

"Dam dam dam," Molly mimicked.

Carrie shot him a disapproving look. "Just know that the day she fires off profanity in public I'm going to walk away as quickly as possible, leaving you to explain where she learned it."

"You don't get much practice controlling your tongue in a military platoon," Noah defended. "I'm working on it."

"I appreciate that. A chubby-cheeked one-year-old who curses like a sailor is only so cute." Reaching for something in Molly's hand, she said, "What did you find, baby?"

Before Noah could stop her, she'd pulled the VA letter from between the couch cushions.

"Nothing," he said, snagging the paper from Carrie's hand. "Junk mail."

"Noah, that's VA letterhead. What's going on?"

Darting off the couch, he said, "I told you. It's nothing."

"If it was nothing you wouldn't be so determined to hide it," she said, following on his heels. "We can't make this work if you shut me out. You don't have to let me read it, but at least tell me what it's about. It isn't anything bad, is it?"

Knowing she was right, he stopped just inside the kitchen. "Did I ever tell you that I got out of the service nine months before I actually came back here?"

She shook her head. "No, you didn't. Where were you?"

"Bethesda. Thanks to my *disorder*, as soon as I got out, they put me into a study for a new PTSD drug." Folding and unfolding the paper, he said, "In the end, I didn't actually get the drug. They gave me a placebo for six months, like I was nothing more than a lab rat. The lucky bastards who got the pill got better. For a while. The rest of us got nothing."

"I'm sorry," she said. "So they put you through the hell that created the problem, and then only pretended to offer help."

"That sums it up." Noah tossed the letter on the counter before leaning in the doorway. "Now they want me to do another study. Some pill and psychotherapy mix."

"Does this one look more promising?" Carrie asked.

"Hell if I know. I'm not getting poked and prodded again just to come home as fuc . . . I mean, messed up as I already am."

"But what if this one works? What if this one makes a difference and can give you some peace?"

Noah rubbed his thumb along her cheek. "*You* give me peace. You're the only thing that's made any difference with this thing. So they can shove their study up their—" Before he could finish the thought, Carrie's face lit up, and Noah spun to see what had happened behind him.

"Hellfire. She's walking." Molly took three more steps before losing her balance and dropping to her bottom. Big blue eyes stared up at them with a smile that showed three tiny teeth.

"You did it, baby!" Carrie yelled, sweeping her daughter off the floor. "You want to do it again? Huh?" She put the baby back on her feet near the couch. "Go on, hon. Go get Noah."

Arms stretched wide, Molly put one foot in front of the other and made it within a foot of the doorway. Noah lifted her off the ground before gravity could claim the victory. "That's my girl. I knew you could do it."

"She is your girl," Carrie said, eyes misty. "And now she's our walking girl. Life will never be the same."

Feeling like the luckiest man alive, he shook his head. "No, ma'am. Life will never be the same again."

Chapter 21

Carrie filled two mugs with hot coffee, heavy cream and sugar for her and black for Noah, before heading outside. Molly had just gone down for her nap, and Noah had to be freezing by now. He'd gone out nearly an hour ago to add caulk around the trailer windows after adding clear plastic on the inside hadn't solved the temperature struggle.

"Why aren't you wearing a coat?" she demanded when she found him at the far window along the back.

"I got hot," he replied, keeping the caulk gun moving in a steady line. "It isn't so bad out here."

"Noah, it's thirty-eight degrees."

"Feels a hell of a lot better than one hundred and twenty."

She couldn't argue with that. "Take a break and have some coffee."

Leaning the tube against the side of the trailer, Noah brushed his hands off on his jeans and took the mug. "She sleeping?" he asked.

Carrie nodded. "I have the monitor in my pocket. It looks like you're almost finished."

"The two on the end and it's all sealed."

Though it was considerably warmer than her trailer, they'd yet to find safeguards for all the baby hazards in Noah's house, which left them no choice but to stay put for now. The stairs alone scared Carrie half to death. In the week since Molly took those first steps, she'd conked her head on each end table, fallen face-first into Wilson's water dish, and even disappeared for what seemed like hours before finally being located behind the couch. Those had been the longest thirty seconds of Carrie's life, and she was pretty sure it was the source behind Noah finding his first gray hair.

Which she wisely said made him more distinguished looking.

"I forgot to pick up cat food at the store yesterday," she said. "Wilson doesn't handle fasting well, so I need to make a quick trip to town when you're finished here."

"That cat could go a week without food and still be ten pounds overweight," Noah said with a chuckle before sipping his coffee.

"I told you—"

"He's big-boned. I got it."

Cradling her mug with both hands, she said, "Can I run an idea past you?"

"What's up?"

"Well," she hedged, nervous what his response might be. "Molly's birthday is next month."

He leaned against the house and crossed one foot over the other. "Yeah. I heard that somewhere," he said with a smile.

Carrie shook her head at the sarcasm. "I want to know what you think about us having her party in the farmhouse."

"In my farmhouse?"

"Yes, *your* farmhouse. It's much bigger than my trailer, and I know I could have a party in town, but then I have to haul stuff all over the place, and it would be so much easier—"

"Go for it," he cut in.

Holding his gaze, she said, "Are you sure? I mean, we aren't talking a hundred people, but there would be a good number in your house."

Noah shrugged as he set his coffee on the back porch rail. "I don't imagine they'll be rifling through my drawers."

"You don't have drawers," she pointed out. "You keep everything on the floor in your closet."

Tapping her on the nose, he said, "Goes to show what you know. I bought a dresser yesterday."

"Really?" He hadn't mentioned buying a piece of furniture. "How did you get a dresser in the house by yourself?"

"Cooper helped me," he said, as if this wasn't the least bit unusual.

Carrie backed up until her bottom hit the porch. This was all too much. She needed to sit down.

"You're hanging out with Cooper now?"

Full lips curled into a crooked grin. "We aren't going steady or anything, but I'm hoping he'll ask me to prom."

"Be serious," she said. "When did this happen?"

Returning to his task, Noah said, "I stopped by his garage last week to see if he could get me a deal on snow tires for your car." Pausing, he added, "They're on order, by the way. He asked about the bikes, we exchanged numbers, and when I needed another strong back, I called him."

Befuddled, Carrie stared at the man she loved as if he'd told her he'd signed up for ballet lessons. "But why didn't he stick around to say hello?"

Shaking his head, he turned her way. "You're a hard woman to surprise, you know that?"

She perked up. "You have a surprise for me?"

"I was going to show you when I was done here." Setting the caulk on the porch, he took her hand. "Come on."

❦

"Slow down," Carrie said. "I want to drink my coffee, not wear it."

He shortened his gait so she could keep up.

"What's the surprise?" she asked.

The woman was worse than a little girl. "If I told you, it wouldn't be much of a surprise."

They trudged through the gate, onto his porch, and into the house, where a wave of warmth hit them in the face.

"Oh my gosh, it's so nice over here," Carrie sighed.

Yes, it was. Which had been the impetus behind the surprise. There would be much left to do, but this was a solid first step to making his house a home.

"Upstairs." He pointed, letting her go first.

Carrie set her mug on the newel at the bottom of the stairs and made her way to the second floor. At the top, she looked to him for guidance, and Noah nodded toward his bedroom. His gut clenched with nerves as she pushed the door open and stepped in.

"Oh, Noah," she said, turning to him with a hand over her mouth. "It's beautiful."

Able to breathe once again, he said, "So you like it?"

"Like it? I love it." Carrie made her way around the room, trailing a hand along the dresser before turning to the bed. "You even got nightstands."

"They all came together. That Snow friend of yours said this is the one you'd want."

She stopped on the other side of the bed. "You talked to Snow?"

Going for honesty, he said, "I can't afford to buy new stuff, and the crap in Ma's attic is ugly. I checked that curiosity shop, and she had this." When Carrie brushed her hands over the comforter, he added, "Snow had that, too. I wasn't sure if you'd like that color blue, but she said it was the right one."

Nodding, Carrie held silent, examining every nook and cranny of the new furniture.

When she touched the curtain, Noah said, "Haleigh sent those with Cooper. He told her what I was doing, and I guess she knew there'd be something a guy would forget."

Carrie stared out the window long enough for doubts to seep into Noah's mind. This had been his way of letting her know that he wanted her here with him. All the time from now on. But he hadn't asked her first. Maybe she didn't want that. Maybe he'd read things wrong and had moved too fast.

"This doesn't have to mean anything," he said, attempting to back-pedal his way to safer ground. "It's just furniture. I had to get some anyway."

"But this *does* mean something, doesn't it?" she said, turning with tears in her eyes. "You bought *me* furniture and put it in *your* bedroom."

Sliding his hands into his back pockets, Noah manned up. "I was hoping it could be *our* bedroom. You know. Eventually."

Running at full speed, she hit him like a runaway freight train, crying what he hoped were happy tears and tucking her face into his neck. Noah held his ground. Barely.

"Is that a yes?" he asked, holding his breath.

Her head bobbed up and down as his shirt collar grew wet.

"Good," Noah said, holding her tight, ignoring the bulky winter coat tickling his nose. "Then that's settled."

If anyone had told Carrie that the moment a man—no, the right man—asked her to spend the rest of her life with him, that she'd be bundled up in a parka and would follow up the glorious moment with a trip to the grocery store to buy food for her morbidly obese cat, she probably would have believed every word of it. Because this was how her life went.

A tragedy one minute. A comedy the next. And now, thanks to Noah, a real love story.

Humming a happy tune as she carried her little blue basket around the store, Carrie smiled at every patron who gave her an odd look. Had they never seen a tiny woman wearing a ridiculously large biker jacket before? She may not have gotten a ring, which she could give two figs about, but she was darn well going to wear something of Noah's to mark the occasion. Since he didn't wear jewelry except his dog tags, which came with a negative connotation in his case, she swiped the jacket. He'd laughed and called her crazy. Which she was.

Crazy in love.

Molly had still been sleeping when Carrie left, but the nap wouldn't last much longer, and she had a future to celebrate, which put an extra pep in her step. Since they weren't the wine-toasting type, she went for ice cream instead, tossing a bottle of chocolate sauce into the basket for good measure. That way Molly could partake in the celebration as well.

Strolling down the pet food aisle, she was picking up a stack of three small cans when something caught her eye farther down the row. There she was. The stranger she'd bumped into at the bananas the day of Lydia's party. Paying little attention to what she was doing, Carrie slid half a dozen more cans into her basket and then faked a deep interest in dryer sheets in order to get closer to the woman. This time she had a distinct purple bruise around her left eye and an ACE bandage around one wrist.

Anger flared to life. This woman needed help. She needed a way out. The shelter wouldn't open for more than a month, but Carrie knew what could happen in that short time. Based solely on their previous encounter, she believed with every fiber of her being that the violence this woman endured would continue to escalate. The bandage would give way to a cast. The bruise to a shattered jaw.

"Excuse me," she said, following her instincts. "Could I bother you for just a second?"

The stranger glanced around, eyes darting with fear. "I don't—"

"I want to switch to a new detergent, but I'm not sure which one to try," Carrie continued, taking extra precaution in case the woman's husband was close by. "Which one do you recommend?"

"I use that one," she replied, pointing to a blue bottle on the shelf.

"I haven't tried that one yet." Carrie stepped closer and dropped her voice to a whisper. "Is your husband here with you?"

She shook her head. "He's out in the car."

"I've been where you are, and I want to help."

"I don't know what you're talking about," the woman muttered, holding a hand near her throat. "I don't need any help."

Undeterred, Carrie said, "My husband beat me for five years. I've had those bruises. And I never found the courage to get out."

Bloodshot blue eyes glanced up and down the aisle. "Are you still with him?"

"A friend helped me get away, and shortly after, my husband died." Being completely honest, she added, "I probably would have gone back to him if that hadn't happened. I'm not sure I'd be alive today if I had. Let me help you. Please."

Dropping her gaze to the floor, the stranger said, "What can you do for me? He'll never let me go."

Searching her purse, Carrie found an old receipt and wrote down her cell phone number. "I'm working with a group to open a shelter on the edge of town, but the renovations are going to take another month.

If you see a chance to get out, call me." She stuffed the paper into the woman's hand. "I'll come get you wherever you are."

Tucking the number into her coat pocket, the woman said, "Where would I go? You just said the shelter isn't open yet."

Offering what Lorelei had given to her, Carrie said, "You can stay with me. Then, when Safe Haven is up and running, we'll move you over there. At least until you find another place to stay. What's your name?"

"Roberta. Roberta Hawkins."

Carrie squeezed Roberta's hand. "Your husband works, right?"

"Yes." She nodded. "He does maintenance at a school in White House."

"Good. Hide some money, pack a bag, and then pick a day you know he'll be home late. Do you understand?"

Hands shaking, Roberta brushed the curls off her forehead. "I don't know if I can do that."

"Roberta!" boomed a voice from the end of the aisle. "What's taking so long?"

"I'm sorry," Carrie said, flashing her most innocent smile. "I'm trying to decide what detergent to switch to, and I'm afraid I begged your wife to help me pick." Adding a detail she knew would appease the monster, she said, "My husband doesn't like the smell of the one I'm using now, so I need to find one he'll like better. We have to keep our men happy, don't we?"

"Tell her what you use," he snapped at his wife.

"The blue one," Roberta answered, again pointing to the second shelf down.

"Then that's the one I'll buy," Carrie said, nearly choking with the need to grab Roberta and run.

"Let's go," the brute grunted, jerking his wife by the arm without giving Carrie a second look. The scared woman glanced back before being dragged out of view.

As her adrenaline ebbed, Carrie began to shake, dropping her basket to the floor as she fought to catch her breath. She had just invited a stranger into her home. A woman she knew nothing about. Except that she was in danger and suffering and in need of a way out. Carrie could give her that way. And when the shelter opened, they would have their first resident. That is, if the woman even called at all.

Taking that step would require a great deal of courage. Something Carrie had never found for herself, but she had the power now to be courageous for someone else. Hopefully, she'd get the chance.

Chapter 22

"Hey, Noah," Jordan said, sticking his head into the room where Noah was mudding the walls. "You're gonna want to come down here."

"Why?" he asked, smoothing the mud into a seam.

"Carrie's here."

Noah lifted the trowel off the wall. "Does she have Meredith with her?"

Jordan shook his head. "Nope. She's by herself, but she isn't empty-handed."

"Payday isn't until Friday. What's she have?"

Scratching beneath his hard hat, the younger man said, "Paintbrushes."

No way he heard that right. "Come again."

"She says she's here to help. She's got rollers and tape and everything."

For the last week, every conversation had turned into a battle over why the shelter couldn't open sooner than the mid-December date. And in every debate, Noah had ticked off a list of perfectly rational reasons that Carrie seemed determined not to hear.

"Well, hell." Dropping the trowel in the hand bucket, he set both on a sawhorse and followed Jordan down the hall to find Carrie wearing faded jeans, one of his stained T-shirts tied in a knot at her waist, and her hair swinging in a ponytail on the back of her head. And damn if he didn't find painter Carrie hot as hell. "I've got this, Jordan."

"Right, boss."

Once the kid shuffled out the door, Carrie said, "Did he just call you boss?"

"Babe, what are you doing here?"

"I'm painting," she said, as if this were an everyday thing. "I know the paint was delivered this morning because I got a delivery notice in my email. So I figured I'd get started."

Digging deep for patience, Noah said, "We have professionals lined up to do that next week."

"But the paint is here," she pointed out. "There's no reason to wait until next week."

"There is if I don't want guys tripping over each other."

"I'm a crew of one, and I'll only paint in the rooms where no work is being done." Pushing two rolls of blue tape onto her arm, she picked up a long-handled roller off the floor. "Now where did you guys put the paint?"

"Honey. You're driving me nuts."

"Get me the paint, and I'll be out of your hair."

"It isn't that simple." Noah rubbed his hands over his face. "This is a construction site. We have safety guidelines we have to follow. You doing the painting breaks about eight of them."

"I'm an employee of Lowry Construction," she argued before knocking on the yellow thing on her head. "I have a hard hat. I'm not using any power tools. I'm not swinging a hammer. And I have safety goggles even though I won't need them to paint. There is absolutely no reason I can't be here."

"Yes, there is," he snapped. "Because I said so."

Dammit. He did not want to lose his temper, but there was no way he could concentrate on anything knowing that Carrie was somewhere on-site doing who knows what and possibly getting hurt.

"Noah, come on," she pleaded. "What's the big deal? It's a little paint."

"Carrie, go back to the office. I get that you want to help, but the best way to do that is to let us do our jobs. Okay? Please."

Leaning the roller against the wall, she let the tape rolls drop to the ground.

"We need this shelter open earlier."

"Why?" he asked. "Why can't this wait four more weeks?"

She opened her mouth, and then closed it again. Eyes darting around the room, she finally said, "It just can't."

"It's going to have to, hon. And as soon as it's done, I'll hand you the keys and you'll be all set to save all the people you can."

Storming past him, she mumbled, "It might be too late by then."

He couldn't fault her for wanting so desperately to help people, but there was only so much Noah could do at this point. At least on the shelter project. But maybe there was something he could do to move the house along. The distraction of setting up a new home might help the next month fly by a little quicker. Pulling his phone from his pocket, Noah fired off a text on his way back down the hall.

Carrie checked her phone twice on the way to Lorelei's house. She'd made sure to keep her battery charged and jumped every time the thing rang. It had been over a week with no word. Sick with worry, Carrie even attempted to search the Internet for any information on a Roberta Hawkins in Ardent Springs. Nothing came up. Which didn't surprise her.

Men like Roberta's husband controlled every aspect of their spouse's life. Limited their contact with friends, if they let them have any at all. Kept them at home so they couldn't possibly make any money of their own. No autonomy. No independence. And above all, no freedom. All while appearing for all the world like a perfectly normal married couple.

There was nothing normal about punching your wife. And every day Roberta didn't call, Carrie feared it would be too late. That one night she'd sit down to dinner and the lead story on the news would be accompanied by a tiny insert image of Roberta's beaten and battered face.

"Are you sure the pink and purple is what you want?" Lorelei asked, pointing to a picture in the magazine in front of them. "The red-and-purple one is cute, too."

"I trust you," Carrie said, too distracted to deal with frosting colors. "Whichever one you like is fine."

"What is going on with you?"

Carrie met concerned blue eyes. "Nothing. There's nothing going on with me."

Lorelei flipped the magazine shut. "Honey, we're talking about your daughter's first birthday cake and you just said whichever is fine."

"We need a clean diaper over here," Rosie called from the couch. "And a whole pack of wipes from the smell of things."

"I'll do it," Carrie said, but Lorelei shoved her back into her seat and carried the diaper bag to her grandmother. When she returned, they picked up where they'd left off. "You've been distracted since you got here, have checked your phone every two minutes, and you haven't touched a single cookie. There's definitely something going on."

Pushing Roberta to the back of her mind, Carrie used the day before as her excuse. "Noah and I had a disagreement yesterday. I guess it's still bothering me."

"Trouble in paradise, huh? Tell Auntie Lorelei all about it."

She toyed with the corner of the magazine. "I went to the shelter with the intention of painting some walls, but Noah wouldn't let me stay."

"Doesn't Mike hire a crew for that?"

"He does," she confessed. "But I thought if I pitched in that we could open the shelter sooner. I don't understand why no one is in a hurry on this. There are women out there who need a place to go."

Patting her hand, Lorelei said, "There will always be women who need a place to go. And in a few weeks, they'll have one."

"Four," Carrie corrected. "Four weeks. Do you know what can happen to a woman in a month's time? What a man can do to her?"

"I prefer not to think about it," her friend admitted. "But I'm sure that the guys are doing their best to get it done. Noah knows it's important to you, and he knows why, right?"

Carrie nodded. "He knows."

"And things are good between the two of you other than this shelter thing?"

"They'll be better when we can move into the house for good, but yeah. We're okay."

Lorelei leaned back in her chair. "You're moving into his house?"

Confused, Carrie replied, "I assumed Snow would have told you."

"Told me what?"

"That Noah bought furniture."

"You're going to have to elaborate on that."

Flashing back to the week before, Carrie smiled at the memory. "Noah's bedroom contained a bed and nothing else. Not even curtains.

So he went to Snow's store and bought a dresser and some nightstands. Plus new bedding. And Haleigh sent some curtains with Cooper, who helped him get it all in when I wasn't around. He surprised me with it."

Trying to follow along, she said, "So Noah bought himself bedroom furniture."

"No," Carrie corrected. "Noah bought *me* bedroom furniture and put it in *his* room."

Still bewildered, the blonde tilted her head, contemplating the last statement. The moment she solved the mystery, Lorelei shot out of her chair.

"He asked you to marry him."

"Without saying a word." Carrie nodded, unable to keep the grin off her face. "It was the sweetest thing anyone has ever done for me."

"Did you hear that, Granny? Carrie is getting married."

Losing control of the situation, she jumped to her feet. "No, I'm not."

Lorelei grabbed her by the arms. "You said *no?*"

"No. I mean, I said yes. But we aren't getting married. Well, someday we'll get married. But not right now."

Rosie carried Molly into the kitchen. "She isn't marrying anyone until I meet him."

"You have met him, Granny," Lorelei said, pulling a yellow notepad from a drawer in the kitchen island. "He's the guy she brought to my wedding."

"I barely got a hello out of that man."

"Noah is shy," Carrie defended.

"He likes my cookies, and he makes Carrie happy. You can get to know him later." Returning to her stool, Lorelei looked up with a pen poised over the notepad. "Summer or winter? Oh, or fall. Fall weddings are wonderful."

Rosie snorted. "She says, completely unbiased."

"I haven't thought that far ahead." Molly dove into her mother's arms, tucking her head against Carrie's neck. "She's tired. We better get home."

"But there are a million more questions."

"Lorelei, let the girl be. She just told you they aren't getting married for a while." Wagging a finger beneath Carrie's nose, Rosie added, "And I haven't given my approval yet."

Carrie attempted to appease the older woman. "I really love him, Rosie. And Molly adores him."

"Well. That's a good sign. Kids can spot a bad penny from twenty paces." Propping her hands on her hips, she said, "Does he really make you happy, sweetie?"

"Very."

"All right then. He's approved. But if he ever hurts you, he'll have a lot of people ready to pounce on his ass."

"Granny!" Lorelei exclaimed. "You'd smack me for saying that."

The protective grandmother put her arm around mother and child. "When it comes to taking care of our own, we don't mess around."

The heartfelt words brought a tear to Carrie's eye. "Thank you, Rosie. You'll never know how much that means to me."

The older woman placed a soft kiss on Molly's cheek. "You're family, honey. Don't ever doubt it."

⌒

"Anyone home?" Noah called as he stepped into the workshop. Despite the cold air, two days of rain had given way to a bright November Saturday, and his eyes struggled to adjust to the change in light levels.

"I'm here," called a voice from his left. "How you doing, man?" Spencer asked, joining Noah near the entrance.

"I'm good. I'm hoping you can help me solve a problem."

"Come on back." He led the way to a slanted work desk on the back wall. "You said something on the phone about building gates. Are we talking fence gates?"

Noah shook his head. "No, I need something that will block Molly from getting up the steps at the house, as well as something at the top to keep her from falling down."

Sliding his hands into his pockets, the carpenter said, "They make baby gates. Why don't you just buy a couple?"

"The farmhouse is about a hundred years old. Those gates aren't wide enough for what I need. And even if they were," Noah added, "I don't trust them. These things have to be sturdy and taller than the standard size so she can't climb over them."

"That's a point in your favor." Spencer took a seat on the stool in front of the desk.

"What's that supposed to mean?" Noah asked, unaware that he was being scored.

"I don't know you, but I know *of* you," he said. "Back in the day, you had a rep for being an arrogant asshole. Add the fact that you were friends with the guy who beat the shit out of Carrie, and that isn't a great first impression."

"Forget I bothered you." Noah headed out the way he'd come.

"But," Spencer said, speaking loudly enough to be heard across the room, "people change. I've seen it firsthand, and according to Lorelei, you really care about my ex-wife. That you take Molly's safety so seriously is another check in your favor, and I respect your service to this country. So if you still want my help, I'm happy to give it."

Appreciating the honesty, Noah ambled back to the desk. "Is that really the rep I had back then?"

"Does it sound like an accurate description?"

Scratching his beard, Noah took a hard look at his teenage self. "Yeah. That's about right."

"You still want my help?" Spencer asked.

Knowing that Spencer cared about Molly's safety as much as he did, Noah nodded.

"All righty then. Let's design some custom baby gates."

Half an hour later, Noah held a drawing of exactly what he'd imagined, only turning the design into reality required a few measurements he hadn't taken. Easy enough to fix once he got home. Before he returned to his truck, Spencer offered a tour of the workshop, which continued into another room that Noah hadn't realized was there. In the middle of the much larger space sat a table that must have been nine feet long.

"Where is that thing going?" Noah asked.

"Cooper's backyard. He's notorious for his cookouts, and every year there seems to be more people. So I'm building this picnic table to hold everyone."

Noah bent down to see the beautiful plane work. "This is nice, man."

"Thanks. I've been working on it for a few months between other jobs. There's no hurry since he won't need it until the spring."

Getting an idea, he said, "I could use a new table in the farmhouse." Even though nothing had happened between him and Kyra, the current kitchen table still carried a bad feeling for Carrie. On the few occasions they'd eaten at his place, she always insisted they sit in the living room. "You willing to build me something custom? I'd pay, of course."

"I'd be glad to do that. You know what you'd want? Oak? Cherry?"

"I've got some reclaimed wood in the barn. Could you use that?"

Spencer rubbed his hands together. "No idea, but I definitely want to see it."

Looking ahead to the coming week, he'd be working late at the shelter for the first half due to the holiday, and then Thanksgiving dinner at his mom's on Thursday. "If you're free next Friday, hit me up and you can come check it out."

"That'll work."

The men finished the tour, and Noah hit the road. He debated whether or not to tell Carrie about the table, and then he considered that she might want a say in what the thing should look like since she'd be stuck with it in her kitchen for a good long while. The thought put a smile on his face. If he played his cards right, they could be in the farmhouse full-time before Christmas.

Chapter 23

Carrie got the call just before noon on Saturday. Thankfully, Noah was away from the house, because she had *no* idea how to tell him what she was about to do. When she'd made the rash offer in the grocery store, all Carrie had been thinking about was getting Roberta to safety. Lorelei had done the same for her, opening her home, and now Carrie would pay it forward. It wasn't as if this were a permanent solution. Once the shelter opened, Roberta would be their first client.

Fully aware that something could go wrong, Carrie had called Lorelei to babysit, using the excuse of wanting to go birthday shopping without Molly along. Acting normal while dropping her off had been difficult, but not nearly as nerve-racking as when she'd reached the address Roberta had given her. By some miracle, the abuser had gone hunting for the whole weekend, secure in the fact that his well-trained wife would never think of leaving him. On the ride home, Carrie had learned that her new friend had been married less than two years and, much like her own experience, had witnessed no signs of violence prior to tying the knot.

It was as if they were all trained by the same master.

Be attentive. Be kind. Be everything she could ever want in a man—until you get the ring on her finger. Then, make sure she understands who's in charge. Keep her in line with fists and threats, always with the reminder that no one else would have her, and that *she's* making you do this to her. Make her listen. Make her obedient. Make her weak.

Bile bubbled in Carrie's throat just thinking about it.

"I can't believe I've done this," Roberta said for the fourth time. "He's going to kill me. When he finds me, he's going to kill me."

Carrie had been pacing the living room for nearly half an hour. Noah would be home any minute, and she had yet to come up with a way to explain why there was a strange woman in her trailer. A strange woman whose violent husband would fly into a rage upon finding her gone. At least they had another day before having to deal with that part.

"Roberta, you have to stay focused here," she said, perching on the edge of the coffee table. "We had to get you out. That was the hard part, right?"

Wringing her hands, the scared woman said, "But what if this man of yours is angry that I'm here? What if he kicks me out?"

"That won't happen. Noah is a good man," Carrie assured her. "He wouldn't put you in danger like that. And besides," she added, "this is my house. His is next door. He couldn't kick you out if he wanted to."

But that didn't mean he'd approve of this spontaneous misadventure either.

"I don't feel safe," Roberta said, hopping off the couch. "If I'm still in town, he'll find me. I need to get farther away."

Hopeful, Carrie followed her across the room. "That's an excellent idea. Do you have a friend or a relative out of state? We can put you on a bus this afternoon."

Roberta shook her head. "I don't know anyone. My late aunt raised me, but she didn't like mixing with people in town. I guess I might have family somewhere, but I wouldn't know how to find them."

And Carrie thought *she'd* lived in a small world. "How did you meet Wayne if you kept to yourself?"

"At the feed store," she admitted. "Granny and I stocked up once a month for the dogs and chickens, and one day Wayne was there, too. He stopped me to tell me I was pretty." She toyed with her hair. "No one had ever told me I was pretty before. I married him a month later."

Don't judge. Don't judge.

"You *are* pretty, Roberta, and you deserve a man who won't lay his hands on you." Carrie heard a car outside and ran to the front window. "Noah is home," she said, frantically closing the blinds. "Hide in Molly's bedroom."

"Why do I have to hide?" she asked as Carrie herded her along. "You said he wouldn't be mad."

"Just give me a few minutes to explain the situation." Something told her this would take more than a few minutes to explain. "Then I'll bring you out, and we'll all sit down and decide what to do next. Okay?"

Nodding, Roberta said, "Okay."

Carrie shut the door and rushed to the kitchen. Flustered, she flipped on the faucet to clean the one bottle in the sink.

Closing the door quickly behind him to keep out the cold, Noah looked around. "Where's Molly?" The baby had taken up the habit of running for his legs whenever he walked into the house.

"With Lorelei," she said. "She hasn't seen her much since they came back from the honeymoon, so I let them have her for a while."

"Them?" Noah asked, setting his keys on the counter.

Scrubbing the nipple, she said, "Yeah. Her and Spencer."

Stopping with his jacket half off, he said, "I was with Spencer, and I didn't see Lorelei or Molly."

Carrie shut off the water. "You were with Spencer?"

"I went to see if he can build a couple custom gates for the stairs over at the house. Top and bottom to keep Molly from crawling up or falling down."

Crisis temporarily forgotten, she said, "That's so sweet. Did he say he could do it?"

Noah shrugged the rest of the way out of his jacket and pulled a folded piece of paper from the pocket. "We think so. But he'll need a couple more odd measurements that I didn't have with me. I'll get those tonight and send 'em over."

"You should do that now," Carrie said, seizing the opportunity for more time. "I have some laundry to finish, and dinner won't be ready for hours. Go on over, and I'll come get you when the chicken is done."

Bracing his hands on the counter edge, he stared her down. "Carrie, what is going on?"

"Nothing," she said, her voice hitting an octave she didn't know she had. "There's nothing going on."

Glancing around the trailer, he said, "Why is Molly's door closed? Are you hiding something?" If his smile was any indication, he assumed the surprise was a good one.

She attempted a natural laugh. "Of course not. I caught Wilson in Molly's crib earlier, so I closed the door to keep him out."

Brow furrowed, Noah said, "How did Wilson get in the crib? He can barely heft himself onto the couch."

"I don't know." She shrugged. "But he was in there."

"You're hiding something," he said, bouncing off the counter. "It better not be a puppy. If I can't get her a pony, you can't get her a puppy."

"Wait." Carrie sprinted across the living room, cutting Noah off before he reached Molly's door. "Okay. I admit it. I'm hiding something. But I don't want to reveal it until after dinner. So stop trying to spoil it."

Noah crossed his arms. "I showed you your surprise early."

Carrie stood her ground. "You did that on your own. I could have waited."

Gripping her shoulders, Noah planted a hard kiss on her mouth. "You're lucky I'm in a good mood. I'll wait."

She sighed with relief. "Oh, thank goodness."

"But when I get back," he said, grabbing his coat, "no more waiting."

"I promise," Carrie said. "All will be revealed when you get back."

Full lips quirked into a sexy grin of warning as he traipsed back outside. Carrie fell against the door behind her only to nearly land on her butt when Roberta opened it.

"Why didn't you tell him?" she said. "This was a mistake, wasn't it? You're afraid of him. I can see it."

"No. No, no, no. That's not it at all." Carrie chased Roberta into the living room. "I'm not sure how to explain this to him, that's all. I mean, I probably should have told him I was going to do this. It sounded much simpler in my head before everything kicked into motion today."

"Carrie, I appreciate you trying to help me, but I don't want to mess up your life. I shouldn't have dragged you into my trouble."

Taking her hands, Carrie pulled Roberta to the couch, forced her to sit, and then did the same. "I put myself in this, and I'm not sorry that I did. We have this one little hurdle of getting Noah on board with us, and then we'll take it one day at a time after that. It's all going to work out."

Looking hopeful, she said, "You really think so?"

More determined than ever, Carrie nodded. "I'm sure of it."

❧

What the hell could she be hiding in there?

Noah pondered the possibilities on his way to the farmhouse. He wouldn't put the puppy thing past her, but he hadn't heard anything moving or yipping through the door, and there was no way Carrie had trained a puppy to be still and quiet in a matter of hours.

Nothing else came to mind. He hadn't asked for anything. Not that he would. Noah didn't need much to get by. His mostly empty house stood as proof to that. Stepping into the warmth, he shed his coat, tossing it on the couch, and passed through to the kitchen for his tape measure. To achieve the gate height he wanted, one side would need to be modified to account for the cut in of the banister. And with the house as old as it was, Noah knew the top and bottom measurements would be different.

With the landing measurement in hand, he started on the bottom. He'd been right. A difference of nearly half an inch. Great-granddad had been a master builder, but even he couldn't account for a century of settling. As the measuring tape snapped closed, Noah heard a noise in the distance. Maybe a carload of teenagers blasting music as they barreled down the back road. The sound came again. Definitely not music.

Leaving the notepad and tape measure on the steps, he crossed to the window and spotted a jacked-up Ford Bronco in Carrie's driveway. A scream cut through the distance as a dark-haired wall of a man dragged a woman out of the trailer. When Carrie chased after him, yelling something Noah couldn't decipher, the asshole spun around, backhanding her hard enough to send her flying through the air.

"Carrie!" Noah roared, slamming his hands against the window the same way he had in his nightmares. But this time the glass cracked. In seconds, he was out the door, clearing the gate with a single leap and dropping his adversary to the ground with an elbow to his nose. The crying woman crawled away as Noah checked on Carrie. The gash across her cheekbone bled onto his hand, and he lost it.

"Get up, you sick son of a bitch." Noah picked the sack of shit up by his shirt, dodging the right hook that grazed his jaw, and with a quick head butt, he sent the asshole stumbling backward.

"That's my wife," the stranger bellowed, pointing at the woman now crying beside Carrie's car. Blood oozed from her nose, and she held her arm as it if was broken. "You and your slut can't keep my woman from me."

Rage ringing in his ears, Noah charged with his shoulder low, sending them both to the ground. The first punch shattered bone. The second shoved his nose into his skull. The image of Carrie taking the hit played over and over in his mind. Never again. He would never let a man hurt her again.

"Noah!" Carrie yelled, pulling him back to reality. "Noah, please. You're going to kill him." She tugged on his shoulders, but he kept punching, oblivious to the shredded skin on his knuckles. "Oh my God, Noah," she cried, her tears getting through to him. "You can't kill him. I won't lose you over this. Please. Stop."

Releasing his grip on the bloody shirt, Noah climbed off the attacker. His hands throbbed, blood speckled his clothes, and Carrie held his face, her cheeks wet with tears.

"Honey? Come back to me, baby. Are you okay?" Frantic, she said, "Is any of this blood yours? Noah, tell me that you're okay."

Too winded to talk, he nodded, touching a fingertip to her cheek. "Don't worry about me. It's just a scratch."

She called that a fucking scratch? The son of a bitch had split her cheek wide open. Fury reignited deep in his gut. Why? Why had she put herself in danger like that? Why had she done something so stupid? And without telling him? Without giving him the benefit of being ready? Of protecting her?

The bleeding man on the ground started to cough.

"Help me, Noah," Carrie said. "He's going to choke on his own blood. We have to roll him over."

Staring at his knuckles, Noah rose to his feet.

"Noah, help me. We can't let him die."

Recognizing the beast gnawing to get out, Noah stumbled toward the fence gate.

"Where are you going?" she called after him, but he kept walking.

He had to get away. Before he did something stupid. Before he lost control.

∽

"Roberta!" Carrie called, struggling to roll Wayne onto his side. "Come and help me. We can't let him die. I will not have his death on Noah's hands."

The battered woman moaned but got to her feet. With her one good arm, she added her strength to Carrie's, and they managed to get her husband onto his side. The coughing stopped, though the bleeding continued.

"Go inside. Get my phone and call 911," Carrie ordered.

"My phone," Roberta mumbled. "That's how he found me. I forgot that he tracks my phone."

They didn't have time for this. "I don't care about that right now. Go in and call 911. And bring me some towels. There's a closet in the hallway. Grab a stack of towels off the shelf." The woman stayed where she was, staring in shock at her husband's face. "Go, Roberta! Do what I told you."

Scrambling to her feet, Roberta limped into the trailer, hugging her left arm close to her body. The moment Wayne had forced his way into the house, he'd shoved Carrie hard enough to send her hurtling across the living room. When Roberta had come to her defense, he'd snapped her arm like a toothpick. Carrie could still hear the crack of the bone, though nothing would ever compare to the sound of Noah shattering the man's face.

Holding her attacker's head off the gravel, Carrie watched Roberta stumble off the porch with a towel under her good arm and a cell phone